A Night on the Town

After dinner Murray's cousin, Richard, stretched and checked his Rolex. "What say we continue our amiable evening at Club Metro? I can get us in."

Thinking he'd impressed us by dropping the name of LA's hottest club—make that hottest, loudest, hipper-than-thou club—he looked for our admiration.

He didn't get it from me. Instead, I yawned. Why would I even want to be seen in a place like that? I totally don't need my hip-cred validated by being seen there. True hipness emanates from within. And from what you wear. As anyone knows.

Addendum: If Daddy found out I was in Club Metro? I'd be toast. A not insignificant postscript. Especially when I'm angling for a new suite of rooms.

I was about to nix the suggestion when Richard dropped the kicker. "My sources tell me Leonardo DiCaprio might be showing tonight."

Before I could revisit my opposition, De screamed, "We are so there!"

Clueless Books

Clueless A novel by • H.B. Gilmour
  Based on the film written and directed by Amy Heckerling
Cher's Guide to...Whatever • H.B. Gilmour
Cher Negotiates New York • Jennifer Baker
An American Betty in Paris • Randi Reisfeld
Achieving Personal Perfection • H.B. Gilmour
Friend or Faux • H.B. Gilmour
Cher Goes Enviro-Mental • Randi Reisfeld
Baldwin from Another Planet • H.B. Gilmour
Too Hottie to Handle • Randi Reisfeld
Cher and Cher Alike • H.B. Gilmour
True Blue Hawaii • Randi Reisfeld
Romantically Correct • H.B. Gilmour
A Totally Cher Affair • H.B. Gilmour
Chronically Crushed • Randi Reisfeld
Babes in Boyland • H.B. Gilmour
Dude with a 'Tude • Randi Reisfeld
Cher's Frantically Romantic Assignment • H.B. Gilmour
Extreme Sisterhood • Randi Reisfeld
Southern Fried Makeover • Carla Jablonski
Bettypalooza • Elizabeth Lenhard

CLUELESS®

Extreme
Sisterhood

Randi Reisfeld

AN ARCHWAY PAPERBACK
Published by POCKET BOOKS
New York London Toronto Sydney Tokyo Singapore

AN ARCHWAY PAPERBACK *Original*

An Archway Paperback published by
POCKET BOOKS, a division of Simon & Schuster Inc.
1230 Avenue of the Americas, New York, NY 10020

®, ™ and Copyright © 1999 by Paramount Pictures

ISBN: 0-671-02092-7

First Archway Paperback printing January 1999

10 9 8 7 6 5 4 3 2

AN ARCHWAY PAPERBACK and colophon are registered trademarks of Simon & Schuster Inc.

Printed in the U.S.A.

IL 7+

QB/✷

Girlfriends rule! Snaps to the über–Extreme Sisterhood: Anne Greenberg, editor-guru; Fran Lebowitz, agent extraordinaire; H. B. Gilmour, author-mentor; Stefanie Reisfeld, world's best daughter; the girlfriend posse at home; and the mother-crew in Queens. Friends all and the best people I know.

Okay, dudes are cool, too—and helped much: Jason Weinstein; Rodger Weinfeld. And of course, Scott Reisfeld, world's best son, and Marvin Reisfeld, world's best spouse, who provided inspiration, sustenance, kvetch-control, and dinner.

And then there's Peabo: Four paws and a constant drool. Thanks for . . . *whatever!*

Extreme Sisterhood

Chapter 1

What exactly is that on your tray, Cher? Ick du jour? It looks like the gunk the contractor used to repair our guest house after El Niño struck."

In one fell swoop, Amber abused my lunch *and* glommed onto us as she snared a seat at our table. We were sitting in the VIP section of the Quad, our school's outdoor foliage- and fountain-enhanced dining area.

Before I could respond, De, who was sitting next to me, snapped, "Didn't you see the sign, Amber? This is a narcissism-free zone. No unchained egos allowed."

Amber ignored her and continued her critique of my lunch. "It looks like you actually got that . . . at the school cafeteria." She glanced at De's tray with equal disdain. "What's yours—the blue plate special?"

I sighed. "We *did* get it in the cafeteria. If you must know, Ambu-snob, our lunch is creatively cutting edge with New Age values. I'm eating tofu cheese with fresh herbs."

De, munching an oat bran muffin, added, "What's your issue, anyway? Ever since Aspen Polotnik's father took over the food concession, the Bronson Alcott High School cafeteria has had solid nutrition cred."

Amber rolled her contact lens–tinted violet eyes. Which matched her shrieking violet—make that *violent*—wig. "Whatever. Some of us choose to cater."

She snapped her fingers. On cue, a waiter approached. "Miss Marins? Your order." He handed Amber a mini shopping bag branded Prego, from which Amber extracted additive-laced chicken fingers and carpaccio.

De snickered. "Of course, *your* culinary choice is so very you. Made entirely of olestra. Like your meaningless, artificial life."

De—Dionne Davenport, that is—and Amber Marins are my nearest and dearest in high school; one by choice, the other by default. I'm just not sure whose fault it is that Amber's always around. But the three of us have been t.b.'s—true blue friends—since archival times. Like, kindergarten.

"Yo, ladies, how goes it this wondrous Wednesday afternoon?" Murray, a wide grin accentuating his 'stache-dappled baby face, greeted us. Momentarily blinded by Murray's screaming citrus satin jacket and matching trou, I had to shield my eyes. That's when I saw Sean. Murray Duvall and Sean Holliday are the Matt Damon and Ben Affleck of our high school—minus the talent.

Instinctively, I slid over, making room for Murray to sit on the other side of De. The longest-lasting love couple in high school, they're like that famous pink TV bunny: they just keep going and going and going. Only unlike that commercial, *they* never get boring. Forever dancing on the precipice of breakup and makeup is their modus oper-romanci. Or something.

Murray's and Sean's lunch trays overflowed with the usual signs of high school boys, a grease-fest of cheeseburgers, double fries and Godzilla-size, sugar-overload sodas. Sean's tray had one unusual side order: the *National Tabloid*.

"Lining for the birdcage?" I guessed. Sean had eclectic reading habits, but rag-mags weren't usually among them.

"Check it out." Sean flashed his trademark megabyte grin and opened the paper to the center-fold. "I had to get the dilly on the two-headed alien family that just landed in Petaluma. It's the *X-Files* in our backyard!"

Murray, furiously fascinated, tried to snatch the mag away from his bud, but De was faster. That star-tled me. Had my main gone all lamebrain? As if! It wasn't the alien exposé that intrigued her. It was the photo op in the column next to it.

"Oooh, look at this, Cher," she cooed. "The McCaughey septuplets! They're having a birthday. Are they beyond sweet, or what?"

"Insulin shock," I agreed, staring over her shoulder. The newsprint color photo was grainy. It muted the hue of the septs' matching outfits, making a kiddie fashion call dicey. But the picture was profoundly precious. It showed the seven little siblings, all sitting in a line.

"This one's Alexis, this one's Joel . . ." De ran down the line of babies.

I chimed in, "That's Kelsey . . . that's Brandon."

Amber groaned. "You actually know their names?" Then she whipped out a twenty-dollar bill and waved it at me. "Here, buy a life."

"Of course we know their names," I responded, "and so should you. Hello, they're part of history!"

De, who was into serious ooohing and aahing, added, "Not to mention soooo adorable. Imagine how much fun they're in for—growing up in their own clique. They'll always have one another. They'll never be lonely."

Murray and Sean had been too busy inhaling their burgers to pay much attention to us, but suddenly Murray's head snapped up. He grabbed De's elbow, alarmed. "But, baby, this infant infatuation . . . it doesn't mean you'd be considering . . . ever . . . a big family . . . personally? Babies cost money. And you know, after we're married . . ."

De shot Murray a virulent stare. "Grievous assumption alert, Murray. And you know what happens when we assume."

"Yeah, yeah," Murray cut her off. "But you gotta think about your girlish figure, baby. . . ."

Wisely, Murray left that sentence unfinished.

"Anyway," De added, "who said anything about *having* children? I just meant it would be fun to grow up in a family with a slew of siblings."

Murray's "whew" was nearly drowned out by Amber's sound-effects-laden faux gagging. "A whole bunch of whiny, attention-grabbing brothers and sisters? Is there anything less appealing?"

De amended, "Good point, Amber. Big families aren't for everyone. The deeply self-obsessed *would* find the burden unbearable."

Amber tapped her sharply manicured fingernails on the table and snarled, "Economics 101, girlfriends. The law of supply and demand. Too many grubby-pawed children to supply in my family, and my personal demands could not be met. Unacceptable."

Sean jumped in. "You're not looking at the bright side, Amber. If there are a lot of kids in the family, you can get away with more stuff. That's how me and my brothers do it—divide up and conquer the parents. That's mathematics 101."

Murray frowned. "Maybe, but with a lot of kids, you gotta put up with the whole competitive thing. Like, say your better-looking brother steals your girlfriend?" He put a possessive arm around De, which she shrugged off.

Amber agreed with Murray. "Or worse—what if your sister snags your haute couture ensemble?"

"In your case, Amber, that would be a favor, not a felony," I noted, indicating her proportion-distortion outfit: miniskirt and ankle-high boots.

De and I did a high five. Then she turned to

Amber. "Whatever. As usual we disagree. Cher and I think it would be cool to come from large families. I have two brothers, but I wish there'd been more of us. And Cher has always wanted at least one sister. Or a brother."

De's speaking for me wasn't wholly out of character. Only she wasn't wholly right. "I don't know, De," I mused. "I think you can be completely fulfilled as an only child."

Amber agreed. "Exactly. Not to mention completely, blissfully spoiled."

Did I just side with Amber? How deeply scary is that?

De's fib radar went up. "Really, Cher? Then how come you play that 'Woe is me, I'm an only child card' when you want sympathy? It has always been such your childhood issue."

De thought she'd nailed me, but not even.

"As if!" I faux huffed. "I play it when I want to get something out of you. Because you always fall for it." I shot her a victory grin, then added, "Besides, Dionne, you and I are the sisters we never had. Which wouldn't be the case if either of us had actual sisters. You don't regret that, do you?"

"But it *is* true, Cher," Amber interrupted, "that you always wanted a brother."

"Only when DKNY came out with a boy line. Otherwise, I'm fully content being an only."

"Wait a minute." De waved a French-tipped finger at me. "You're not getting away that easily. Or do I have to go into our old playhouse and dig out your crayon drawings? Were they not always titled

'Cher's family'? And did they not always show five or six sisters, all lined up on the staircase?"

De saved my childhood drawings? Now *I* dug into my wallet. "While it's damaging to my immune system to agree with Amber, De, you *do* need to buy a life. And segue, I drew all those siblings just so I could put each one in a different designer ensemble. I was six—it was my nascent attempt at wardrobe building."

Murray folded his arms and teased, "Busted, Cher. C'mon, admit it. Even I remember you back in the day—wasn't your favorite book the one with all the sisters? *All of a Kind Family?* Somethin' like that? Tell me I'm wrong: you wished that was your family."

Now I totally huffed. "Excuse me, I liked *Curious George*, too. It didn't mean I secretly longed to be a monkey." In a flash, I reached across the table to cover Amber's mouth. Like that famous poem, better safe than dissed.

For the rest of our lunch break, we fully debated the sibling issue. De and Sean took the more-is-merrier position, citing such supportive siblings as Jane Austen's sisters and—while I would have struck it from the record, based on fiction—the Brady Bunch.

Amber and Murray stuck with the less-is-more side. Their main point seemed to be The multisibling effect always yields a lesser one. They rattled off examples. "Frank Stallone. Joey Travolta. And, hello, untalented Hansons—who among us cannot feel their pain?"

What*ever*. Who would have thought a tabloid photo could lead to an actual debate among normally intelligent teenagers? I heaved a major sigh of relief when the bell for next period rang.

I mean, hello, my t.b.'s are profoundly off the hook about my secret sibling longings. I'm furiously undeprived. Au courant, my life is totally envy-worthy. I live in a fabulous Beverly Hills mini-mansion, with the supremo daddy in the world, who indulges my every material whim. I cite: my closet. Mechanically inclined and operated, it houses a complete collection of every designer known to Bettys the world over. I have an accessory nook that shelves my shoe, chapeau, backpack, tote, and slingback collections. What more could I want?

And that cliché about a lonely only? As if. Okay, so numerically speaking, my family *is* minimalist, since Mom died when I was a baby. But in my case, another cliché applies: You can pick your friends but not your relatives. And I choose stellar t.b.'s. My friends are such my life. With me, De, Murray, Sean, and even Amber, it's all, "Don't hate us because we're a Tommy Hilfiger commercial come to life." The vibrant ads where a group of excellently clad, hygienically correct teenagers congregate in some smog-free sunny environment, looking bodaciously healthy and happy? That's us. I mean, we debate and disagree sporadically, but mostly? We bond. We support. Our lives are way in array.

In conclusion, there's nothing I want for that I don't have.

Except a bigger bedroom.

Chapter 2

That I needed larger personal space dawned on me after school, when, on a whim I decided to unearth those childhood drawings De described. I'd kept some, too. The upper echelons of my live-in closet were the likely location. That's where I keep stuff I would never toss but hadn't looked at in a decade or so. So I dragged a step stool over, intending to fully forage.

But before I took one step up? Hello, unexplored outfit! Right before my eyes was a majorly worthy Dolce & Gabbana ensemble I haven't worn this semester. How could my computer have missed it? Wondering if it still looked chic, I tried it on. And then I saw another and like another and okay, I got side-barred. I never did look for the ancient Crayola-ings.

Instead, I decided to take full inventory of my

stuff. A way excellent idea. I found ensembles I didn't know I owned. Which led to a dilemma: where was I going to put next season's collection? A bigger room is a necessity.

Or maybe . . . Brainstorm! I could move to another wing of the house, fully make it my own. Create my own study alcove, guest bedroom, library, dressing room, jacuzzi nook. It could be the Cher wing!

Nothing—nothing!—pumps me more than a potential project. I was abubble with enthusiasm, aboil with ideas.

I barely noticed how much time had passed when Daddy came home from work. By then there was this Mt. Everest of ensembles on the floor of my room. With me behind it.

"Cher? Are you under there somewhere?" I heard Daddy's dulcet yet weary tones before I saw him.

I poked my head up and grinned. Like Robert Redford, Daddy has fully withstood the test of time—he's rugged. Unlike the Hugo Boss suit I'd prepared for him this morning. It was ragged. Wrinkles ruled. I made a mental note to E-mail Hugo about that.

Even burdened with unsightly creases, Daddy is such the imposing figure. In the courtroom, he's Mel Horowitz, Lion King of litigators. But at home he's litigator cub. If you know how to manipulate him.

"Front and center, Daddy," I answered, standing up so he could see me.

"I shudder to ask what you're doing," he said, surveying the mess and making a face. "But I know you're going to tell me, anyway."

"Duh, Daddy—inventory! Half the stuff in here I've barely worn. So I was thinking, a bigger room, or better, a *suite* of rooms is the solution."

Daddy shook his head benignly. "Well, while you're thinking, think about this. It's almost seven. Be down in the dining room in half an hour. I ordered dinner, and it should be here by then. It's your turn to set the table."

"I'm all over it," I replied, flashing him a fully congenial smile.

Daddy is beyond cute, an opinion not solely based on being his daughter. A parade of appropriately aged Bettys has tried over the years to hook him. But between bringing up Cher and his über-demanding career, Daddy hasn't had time to focus on love. Plus, he hasn't met the right Betty yet.

Until he does, it's my job to be his junior associate and escort for all major disease-oriented charity functions. Like the one that's coming up next month. It's the weekend-long celebratory premiere of Rancho Hot Springs. A combination resort, spa, and New Age retreat, it's full-service, cutting edge, and location-resplendent in upscale Santa Barbara. That other famous spa, LaCosta, will fully have to advertise in hieroglyphics, it'll be so ancient news. The gala grand opening, to benefit some trendy charity, will be attended by the hoi *and* the polloi. It's fully major.

Reminder alert! I've barely started to plan for it.

I abandoned my ensemble-inventory chores to

start my to-do list. I'd just started making columns for evening wear—formal chic vs. evening wear—casual chic when my phone rang.

De sounded beyond bummed. "Gotta bail on our imminent plans, Cher."

Instantly, I knew what she was referring to—and I was surprised. We'd planned this boy-free, girlfriend-bonding weekend: slumber parties, shopping, chick-flick videos, major munchies, and more shopping. Besides De, I'd invited the rest of our clique, Megan, April, Baez, Felice, the two Tiffanys: Gelfin and Fukiyama. Plus, eternal fifth wheel Amber.

For De to cancel, something had to be furiously foul. An emergency ski weekend with her family was my first guess, but not even.

"It's Murray," she informed me. "His cousin Richard is coming for the weekend."

"And the reason that affects our plans would be . . . ?"

De heaved a major sigh. "Cousin Richard is the family's golden boy. Ivy League business school, investment banker to be—he's only twenty and planted on the fast track to success."

"What am I missing here, De? I bow to cousin Richard's eminence, but I fail to see how it involves you."

De lowered her voice conspiratorially. "Murray's always been intimidated by Richard. So he asked me to go shopping with him Friday after school. He needs a seriously stellar outfit. My presence is also requested at this big family dinner the next night."

I frowned. "It almost sounds like you're married to him, De." The minute I said that, I felt remorse. It sounded so petulant. So not me.

De let it go. "It's just for support. You can understand that, Cher."

I could, I supposed. But the concept of a girl-bonding weekend without my main? Not even. "No worries, De. But I'm postponing the weekend plans. All meaning is stripped if you're absent. I'll call everyone and we'll reschedule."

I could practically see the luminous smile lighting up De's face. "You're the best, Cher."

"It's fully *nada,* girlfriend. What are sisters—virtual or biological—for?"

The second I hung up, I scrambled down the stairs to set the table. Even though it's just the two of us, Daddy insists on dinner in our formal dining room, citing some archival ritual from his back story: "We ate every meal in the kitchen when I was a kid. You know why?"

Rhetorical question alert.

"We didn't have a dining room, that's why. We lived in a four-room apartment."

Not using the dining room *would* be tragic. Like the rest of our home, it's all Best Achievement in Set Design. A precisely imprecise Tufekkian Tibetan carpet covers the stained wood floor, objets d'art line the walls, and a Venetian glass chandelier hangs over a huge cherrywood table. As Daddy always reminds me, it was the first important piece of furniture he and Mom bought together.

There *is* one heinous design flaw—albeit temporary. Recently, as some sort of parent joke, Daddy posted an electronic sign on the wall, titled Cher's Gross National Product. Its digital tally increases daily. For Today's Contribution it read: "$1000." Hello, that was yesterday's. When De and I hit Via Rodeo after school. Whatever. Like, très amusing.

Although Daddy's too busy to cook and I was born without the domestic gene, we don't suffer from home-cooked-meal deprivation. We eat in every night—by virtue of ordering out. Tonight's comfort-food feast was courtesy of the Palm, one of Daddy's generation's favorite power restaurants.

Over dinner I fully encouraged Daddy to unburden about his day. Not that I'm vaguely interested in depositions, repositories, and cross-examinations. But getting Daddy to relax and open up is furiously healthful for his overworked soul. Plus, a relaxed, calm Daddy equals a generous Daddy, essential for my new suite of rooms.

I divulged the need-to-know details of my day, including the A I got on my history test and the B-for-effort grade in PE. On the heels of Daddy's "I'm so proud of you," I segued seamlessly into my boda-cious design idea for the Cher Suite.

"You would agree, Daddy, that the west wing of our house is grossly underdeveloped. It stands alone, unused, unloved, neglected. A fate not suffered by other rooms in our house. We use the dining room even though it's just the two of us."

By that point we were on dessert, and Daddy was enjoying the last drop of his crème brûlée. I intuited noncompliance with my idea. So I threw in a kicker: "And, bonus, Daddy—if I get a new suite of rooms, I promise to keep my personal space clutter-free. The cleaning service will barely have to touch it."

Tragically, Daddy remained unconvinced of my grievous need.

"Cher, you already have the biggest bedroom in the house. And that's even without counting your bathroom, your closet, and that anteroom next to it where you keep the Imelda Marcos collection of shoes. How much more personal space could you possibly need?"

I sighed. Daddy is such the male of the species. Men never get it. "Granted, Daddy, I do have what some would consider ample space. But what about my new stuff? What about Tiffany Lerman's cutting-edge Chester handbags? What about Laundry?"

"What's wrong with the laundry room?" Designer-impaired, Daddy was flummoxed.

I rolled my eyes. "Not dry-cleaner-bound stuff, Daddy. Laundry by Shelli Segal, only one of the most cutting-edge fashion designers around. We are so millennium bound, ergo, so many new designers have arrived. Stella McCartney. Gabriele Sanders. Daryl K. Lane Davis. You wouldn't want me to fall behind, would you? I mean . . . I am . . ." I tilted my head and did that puppy-dog thing with my eyes. "Your only little deduction."

Daddy shot me an adoring look. He was so there. To preserve the daddy-daughter moment, impulsively I said, "Guess what? My girlfriend-bonding plans imploded—I'm free on Saturday night. I propose a father-daughter shopping spree. You need a new wardrobe for the Rancho Hot Springs weekend. We could hit Barneys, check out the new Zegnas, Calvins . . ."

Daddy wiped his chin and shook his head. "I'm sure those guys are tops, sweetie, but I can't go with you this Saturday. I have a date—"

"Debrief!" I commanded before he could finish the sentence. Daddy has a date was we-interrupt-this-program news.

Okay, so what Daddy told me wasn't earth-shattering. The clues were in the way he sounded—and the way he looked—during his terse explanation. This date? No random excursion. This had potential. I was psyched!

The short version: Her name was Melissa Hellinger. Amendment: Melissa Hellinger, attorney at law. But when Daddy first knew her, she was Melissa Kronk, fellow student at UCLA law school. Earlier this week, they'd bumped into each other and decided to get together to rehash old times.

Right. As if the short version ever tells the story.

The longer version had to be cajoled out of him. "She was more than a classmate," I guessed.

Daddy cleared his throat self-consciously. "Of course, Cher, this was before I met your mother. Several years before, in fact. And yes, Melissa and I dated."

"Duration of dating phase?" I sounded like the proto-attorney I'll never be, clipped, demanding. But this was furiously crucial info.

Daddy grinned. "I don't know, Cher. A year, maybe."

Hello, he so *did* know. "A year! That's huge. Then what happened? You met Mom?"

Daddy clasped his hands and sighed. "No. Melissa actually met someone—"

"She *dumped* you?" I was viciously incredulous. How could anyone dump Daddy? He's such the catch!

"Look, Pumpkin, it wasn't that traumatic. I mean, maybe back then it was, but it all worked out for the best. I met your mother a few months later. And that was the end of it. I really haven't thought about Melissa in years."

"And now—she's suddenly on the scene?"

I was wary. I couldn't help but reflect on a spuriously similar situation a few months back. His name was Jake. Out of nowhere, he entered my life, masquerading as my soul mate. He made me fall for him, but what he really wanted was access to Daddy, to get revenge for some perceived injustice. Jake completely deceived me.

Daddy reassured me that his situation bore no parallels to mine. He'd run into his old flame at some task-force meeting. He'd recognized her. She's a partner in a law firm in the San Fernando Valley. Since her practice is mainly limited to low-profile domestic dilemmas—adoptions, missing children, custody suits, divorces—she and Daddy had never crossed professional paths.

Until this task force thing earlier in the week. I didn't have to ask what had happened to the guy she'd dumped Daddy for. "She's been separated for two years, officially divorced for one," Daddy advised. "She's ready to start dating again."

"And there you are, at the starting gate." I smiled, feeling warm and mushy all over. Grown-ups could be so cute.

"Who knows, Cher? It's just one date. We'll see."

Chapter 3

*O*kay, so Saturday night at home. Some Bettys would be, "How pathetic is that?" But me? Not even. I mean, it's not *habit*-forming. And, vital point: it's by choice. After I made the cancel calls to all involved in our girlfriend-bonding weekend, my going-out possibilities abounded. My popularity affords me multi options. Yet, the option to stay home was the one that appealed.

My to-do list fully overfloweth. Which conflicted with my I-have-no-time-to-do-it time frame. Ergo, Saturday presented itself as the obvious solution. I planned to indulge in a rare grease-fest from Johnny Rockets—or Ed Debevic's—and then do a full tour of Casa Horowitz's neglected west wing. I sensed that architects would be needed. If I'm going to take over that wing, it might as well be feng shui–correct.

Okay, not that Daddy has exactly stamped

"approved" on the venture yet. But he would. I was so sure that after a mall troll on Saturday afternoon, I went on-line, searching for architects with feng shui–cred. By 7 P.M. I'd filled my virtual shopping cart with several enticing possibilities. I was about to start examining them more closely when my phone rang.

It was De, breathless. "Get dressed. You're joining us for dinner."

"I am? But isn't tonight the big chow-down with Murray's family?"

"Change of plans," De announced briskly. "We're going out. Me, Murray, Richard—"

"And me? With Richard? When did I become blind-date bait?"

"You're not!" De objected. "It's just to round out the . . . foursome."

De's voice descended into pleading decibels. "Please, Cher. I'll do anything you ask—just do me this solid. I need you to be there. Friday night dinner was torture. Murray's father treated Richard-the-striver like He Who Must Be Emulated. It was clear he expects Murray to measure up to the golden boy. And Murray feels inadequate."

That scenario was hard to picture. Murray's self-confidence is like, legendary. At school, anyway. Apparently at home it's a different matter.

"Cher, it was grievous." De continued, "With each passing all-praise-Richard minute, I felt Murray's ego shrink a little more."

Gifted, gorgeous, gregarious, going far—okay, goofy—Murray, a victim of ego shrinkage? I could not wrap that around my brain.

De didn't give me a chance. She fully whined, begged, and cajoled me to come along. "I cannot endure another night like that. So I suggested we take a break from the elders, go out to dinner instead. But even so, I can't support Murray all by myself. I need bolstering."

Sighing, I turned off the computer. Like, a friend in need and all that. "Well, okay, I guess. I mean, Bolsters R Us, at your service. I'll come—if it's as severe as you represent."

"You have no idea, Cher."

Okay, so later? I got the idea. It was all like, Pompous, thy name is Richard. Why hadn't De approached Amber instead of me? She was such the better match for Murray's cousin. At least on the obnoxious meter.

It started ticking around 9 P.M. when they arrived to pick me up. I assumed we'd go in Murray's car, a righteous Beemer convertible. But as soon became obvious, anything Murray had didn't cut it in Richard's world.

The golden cousin was behind the wheel of a fierce limited-edition Jaguar XK8. As he leaned over to open the door for me, he was all, "I know what you're thinking, Cher."

He does? He doesn't even know me, let alone what I could be thinking. Still, I politely let him finish.

He did—smarmily. "But no, the car isn't leased. I do own it."

With that, Richard winked at me and pulled out of

our driveway. Since I had no choice but to sit next to him—De and Murray had distanced themselves by claiming the backseat—I was able to keenly observe and compare the cousins.

The survey said: where Murray was baby-face cute, Richard was sculpted-cheekbone handsome. While, thanks to De, Murray had ditched his screaming citrus attire for the understated cool of Polo, Richard's Nino Cerutti suit over a Perry Ellis T-shirt firmly established his college polish. His one fashion flaw was an ascot. It brought an inevitable Bryant Gumbel comparison to mind. No wonder Murray's dad liked him. He seemed like a peer.

But Richard wasn't just Murray's family's golden boy. He was way worse—totally in touch with his inner jerk.

Discreetly, I managed to swing around and roll my eyes at De to convey "I see what you mean, and you owe me big time for this."

Of course in one area Murray had it all over Richard: personality. While Murray was a sweet, adorable, generous doll, Richard was an annoying braggart. And worse? Unlike other annoying braggarts we've come to know, Richard wasn't covering up for any deep-seated feelings of insecurity. He owned his superiority complex, free and clear.

Richard hadn't noticed my nonverbal exchange with my buds. But how could he? His idea of introducing himself was a monologue of minutiae: stuff about himself he thought I'd want to know. Stuff that made Murray look young and inexperienced.

Within the first ten minutes of our faux date, he

managed to drop names like Buffy drops vampires. While poor Murray had to slag it out in public school, Richard had prep school pedigree, where his career in networking began. He graduated among several scions of the rich and political. Then he was accepted to Stanford University. He got early admission to their business school. And yes, don't bother to even ask, since—*boring*—everyone does, he *is* an FOC man.

Before De could stop me, I ventured, "FOC? Is that a fraternity?"

At first simply haughty, Richard dove into condescend overload. As he slowed to stop for a light, he was all, "A fraternity? No, Cher, when you get to college you'll learn that frats are usually named with letters from the Greek alphabet. FYI—that's 'for your information'—an FOC, as it applies to a Stanford student, means Friend of Chelsea."

He paused just long enough for me to come to a full boil.

Then he made it worse. "Chelsea Clinton, of course."

Through clenched teeth, De leaned forward and hissed, "She knew that, Richard. Just like Murray and I did last night."

Okay, so the fact that Richard knew Chelsea, taken by itself, *was* enviable. I mean, hello, who doesn't want to know what our country's way admirable First Daughter is really like? But Richard wore his pretentious attitude like some badge of honor. No way would I give him the satisfaction of knowing he impressed me.

Which didn't deter him from trying.

"Gotta tell you kids," he droned on as he pulled onto Melrose Avenue, "the best thing about spending the weekend here is getting a break from all those Secret Service agents. What a trial!"

Not unlike the one we're enduring this evening. That's what my second look said to my buds. While Murray remained uncharacteristically cowed, De tried to cut into Richard's relentless bragging.

"So, did you have someplace specific in mind for dinner, Richard, or are you majoring in aimless driving?"

Murray nudged her with his knee, but Richard didn't pick up on the sarcasm intended. Tragically, he reacted as if De had just given him more license to boast.

"Funny you should ask, Dionne. I thought we'd hit the commissary."

I reviewed my mental restaurant index: I didn't know the Commissary. Nor did De or Murray. Richard filled us in. "The Paramount commissary, that is. It happens to be open tonight because there's a showbiz industry function only insiders know about."

No one wanted to ask how Richard came by this tidbit. Not that he gave us a chance. Nonchalantly, he dropped, "Fred Savage—the actor? The one who stars on TV in *Working*? He's a Stanford man. He's in my business ethics class. When I mentioned to Freddy that I'd be in town this weekend, he slipped me the password. Voilà, kiddies, we're in."

For some bizarre reason, Murray suddenly came

to life. Silent Boy yelped, "We're in? On the real, man, that's cool! They do *Star Trek: Voyager* here. Beam me up!"

Okay, so like maybe it *would* have been righteous to dine where no Bronson Alcott Betty could get in before, but the fact that *Richard* got us in cast a pall on the experience. It was all the corollary: Being with him just made De and me want to hate everything, from the white latticework-cum-leafy-palms design statement, to the faux garden alcove we were seated in. As for seeing spaceships, stars, or treks of any kind? Not even. The only other humanoids in the commissary were civilians: crew members and junior execs who got stuck working on Saturday night.

Yet Richard acted as if he'd gotten us backstage at the Oscars. Over shrimp risotto, trendy salads, and steaks, the golden cousin crowed on. De and I tuned him out. But I couldn't help noticing something truly alarming. Murray was actually listening. More like lapping up every draining detail Richard deigned to lay on us.

There was one proper aspect to dinner in the commissary: speedy service. By 11:30, we were ready to be audi.

Alas, any hope for an early wrap was soon dashed. After dinner Richard stretched and checked his Rolex. "What say we continue our amiable evening at Club Metro? I can get us in."

Thinking he'd impressed us again by dropping the name of LA's hottest club—make that hottest, loudest, hipper-than-thou club—he looked for our admiration.

He didn't get it from me. Instead, I yawned. Why would I even want to be seen in a place like that? I totally don't need my hip-cred validated by being seen there. True hipness emanates from within. And from what you wear. As anyone knows.

Addendum: if Daddy found out I was in Club Metro? I'd be toast. A not insignificant postscript. Especially when I'm angling for a new suite of rooms.

I was about to nix the suggestion when Richard dropped the kicker. "My sources tell me Leonardo DiCaprio might be showing tonight."

Before I could revisit my opposition, De screamed, "We are so there!"

A half hour later, we so were. Club Metro was everything I'd imagined it to be and more—for all the reasons I'd never wanted to go there. The lighting was profoundly unflattering, totally dark and smoky. The latter wasn't done with stage effects, but in flagrant defiance of the No Smoking law, due to the proliferation of cigar fumes. Richard, who had no trouble getting us past the bouncer, produced a pair of stogies—one for himself, one for Murray.

De, mindful of her boo's health—and, hello, the law—tried to stop him from smoking it. In any other circumstance, she would have been successful, but this one featured Richard, who mocked, "What's she, your mother, man? You let her tell you what to do?"

Richard had fully impinged Murray's independence—setting the stage for a full-out De-Murray dukes-up contretemps. But not this time. My main knows the fine art of picking her battles. So, with a "whatever," she dropped it. I squeezed her elbow, whispering, "Good move, De—it's only one cigar. Permanent damage, except to the odor sure to be embedded in our ensembles, is fully moot."

Not that De could hear one word I whispered. The decibel level was beyond Metallica concert. As my eyes adjusted to the smoke-filled room, I realized Club Metro was way fire hazard. Three times as many people as could fit were squeezed in. And hello, none of them appeared to remotely resemble Leonardo DiCaprio, or even an impersonator. Club Metro was wall-to-wall wannabes: the full comple-ment of I-wanna-be-cool, wanna-be-seen crowd was here. Most of whom had to shout to be heard above the relentless sledgehammer rock. So not my scene.

At least the eardrum-shattering racket served one worthy purpose. It drowned out Richard. But after like fifteen minutes I yearned for a soupçon of serenity. I considered motioning for De to join me in the ladies' room—but in a place like this? Not even. Who knew what we'd find there? Sludge on the sinks, toilet-paper-challenged stalls, no hygienically correct hot-air hand dryers. Hello, probably no mois-turizing soap at all, let alone those little spray bottles of scent available in better public rest rooms.

So I opted to stick it out at our table. When the waiter came over, waving his pad at us, shorthand for "Can I take your order?" I asked for something soothing. Preferably, a light-froth, skimmed milk, double-decaf latte.

Richard smirked and snorted, "Does this place resemble Starbucks to you, Cher?" To the waiter, he said, "Four Cosmopolitans, my good man."

Okay, so I wasn't sure what a Cosmopolitan was—I didn't think Richard was asking for copies of my favorite magazine—but something told me it was an age-inappropriate beverage. I was about to bring that up when Richard added, "Make them nonalcoholic . . . for now." He nudged Murray with his elbow and said loudly, "We'll come back without the high school girls."

I don't know if it was in reaction to Richard's remark, to head off what would surely be De's postal, or just the smoke accumulation, but suddenly I began to cough uncontrollably. Worse, my eyes started to tear, jeopardizing my stellar makeup application.

De was torn—part of her was ready to go medieval on Richard, but another part knew she *had* to get me to the ladies' room, stat. Mid coughing fit, I jumped up and tugged at her sleeve, ensuring that the better part won out.

Okay, so in retro? The best move probably would have been to dash across the street and hit the facilities at the Sunset Marquis hotel. But that's why they call it hindsight. Without that benefit, blindly we rushed into the club's bathroom. There my worst fears materialized. If the wannabes were all in the main room, the fringe element had staked out the ladies' as their turf.

The bathroom itself was massively microscopic. The three girls already in it made it a crowd. All looked like victims of hostile makeovers. Okay, so except in the case of Amber, I'm usually way too polite to comment, but hello, leather pants work only when paired with a camisole or something suitably girly-soft. Which a bustier wasn't. And the concepts that big hair is back, glow-in-the-dark lipstick is a fashion statement, raccoon makeup is in, or smoking is sophisticated, are the epitome of un. Especially the last, since it spreads the nasty health hazard of second-hand smoke.

I *had* to say something. But which girl to address my remarks to? The one in the bustier had a good four inches on me; Raccoon Eyes in the stilettos had clearly been working out. So I fixed my gaze on the least threatening: a green-eyed blond who'd copied—unsuccessfully—from the Gwen Stefani school of style. Like the righteously nonconformist leader of No Doubt, this girl was decked out in drawstring fatigue bottoms, scuffed ankle-high boots, and a seriously creased crop top, which drew attention to her belly ring. Her chin-length hair was tied in random ponytails. And in case anyone still didn't make the connection, she'd painted a heinous dot on the bridge of her nose.

As politely as I could, I took a step toward her and gave my discourse on the hazards of second-hand smoke, especially in such cramped quarters. I cited statistics from the surgeon general, *Elle* magazine's new survey, and reminded her of the "do unto others" thing.

The cohorts traded startled looks—in a threatening kind of way. The faux Gwen struck a pose and did a discourse of her own: "If you can't stand the smoke, get outta the girls' room." Then she sucked her cigarette deeply, leaned in toward me, puckered her lips—and blew smoke right in my face!

Which made me cough even harder *and* caused instant mascara meltdown. "You heard her," Glow-in-the-Dark Lipstick snarled. "That was your invitation to leave."

Okay, so based on the three-versus-two odds, I was about to turn and make screech marks as I left. But not De. Already ticked off, thanks to Richard's incendiary rudeness, De balled her fist and drew her arm back, ready to haul one on the dot right between faux Gwen's eyes.

I caught her just in time, using every ounce of strength to pull her out of the ladies' room. Angrily, De demanded, "What's with you, Cher? Don't let her intimidate you. Stand up for yourself—or better, let me do it for you."

Gulping for air, I aimed for calm. Both of which were challenges. "Think, De," I finally managed. "Is she really worth ruining your manicure for? We'll never see her again."

Okay, so later, I would think: famous last words.

Or more to the point: wishful thinking.

Chapter 4

When we got back to our table, Murray and Richard were mid-guffaw. Plus, the waiter had just delivered our drinks. Translation: we weren't leaving so soon. Not that it was late. I mean, 12:30 on a Saturday night isn't technically beyond curfew. Pretending it was, however, could facilitate an escape.

Casually, I pulled out my cell phone and dialed Daddy. Secretly, I hoped he'd be all, "What's all that noise? Where are you, Cher? Get home now!" But tragically, Daddy didn't say that. He didn't say anything. Because he wasn't home.

Frowning, I folded my cell and stuffed it into my Prada slingback. I whined, "It's after midnight. Why isn't Daddy home?"

De, still steaming from Richard's patronizing attitude and our tough-chick encounter in the bathroom, barely heard me. Her eyes flashing, she made exaggerated motions of pulling out her compact and reapplying her lipstick.

It was Richard who went for the diss. "Uh-oh—Daddy broke curfew! Gonna put him under house arrest, Cher?" A quasi-quip that Murray found beyond clever. He slapped five with his cousin.

Okay, so when exactly during the course of the evening did Murray begin to bond with him? I mean, weren't De and I here to provide an ego shield for Murray? It appeared those services were no longer required.

It was like, past 2 A.M. when Richard, De, and Murray dropped me home. The minute we turned into the driveway, I saw it: the spot where Daddy usually parks his car was empty. I hit the garage door opener, hoping to find his Mercedes safe and sound inside. It wasn't. I bounded into the house and checked the voice mail messages, but there were none from Daddy. Concerned, I punched in his beeper number.

Within seconds, he called back—way alarmed. "Cher—are you all right? What's wrong?"

I was flummoxed. "Am *I* all right? Hello, I'm the one who's safe at home. Where *are* you? Do you even know what time it is?"

There was shocked silence on Daddy's end. In the background, I thought I heard the sound of waves. As in, the ocean.

Then he cleared his throat self-consciously. "I . . . wow! I guess I didn't realize the hour. The time must have slipped by." He paused. "You were worried about me? Pumpkin, that's sweet but unnecessary."

"Of course I was worried, Daddy. What could you be thinking, staying out so late without even a call? I just got home, and when you weren't there . . . you can't imagine the horrors I've been picturing!"

Okay, that was laying it on thick. I hadn't been picturing any horrors. But a little guilt goes a long way toward the Cher wing. And hello, I rule at playing that card.

Chastised, Daddy promised to come right home.

By the time he did, I'd already scrubbed any residual traces of smoke off myself, changed into pajamas, and positioned myself on the bottom step of our staircase, facing the front door. Which is exactly the spot I often find Daddy in, after summoning *me* home from a curfew-breaker. At those times I come through the door with, like, my head down and affect major contrition, angling for a light sentence. But did Daddy show even a soupçon of remorse, now that the tables were turned? Not even.

Instead of being embarrassed, chagrined, or even the least bit contrite about stressing me out, he was glowing! In a fully ear-to-ear, eyes-lit-up, tie-loosened, suit-jacket-tossed-over-his-arm kind of way. And totally bizarrely, he was whistling a Jurassic classic, "The Way We Were."

What's *that* about? I haven't seen Daddy this buzzed since . . . since . . . well, not ever.

Warily, I tilted my head and scooched over on the step. Grinning, Daddy sat down and gave me a peck on the head. "Sorry to worry you, Cher. Can't imagine how the time got away from me."

Okay, he sounded neither sorry nor unknowing. I shrugged. "Well, Daddy, you know what they say, 'Time flies when you're psyched.' So I guess tonight was a major psych event. You seem totally pumped."

Daddy leaned back on his elbows and stretched his legs out. "I don't know about pumped or psyched, but I did have a really good time tonight. A really *great* time. I just don't think I've ever connected with someone that quickly, especially not on a first date."

Sagely, I noted, "I guess it's because it wasn't a first date. Not technically. I mean, you and Melissa used to go out."

Daddy laughed and got a faraway look in his eyes. "Used to. What's the statute of limitations on 'used to'? That was close to twenty-five years ago. When you start all over again, after all that time, I imagine it should feel like a first date. You know, awkward small talk . . ."

"But it didn't?"

He put his arm around me. "Not for one minute."

Daddy bolted upright. "I know it's late, but by any chance, are you in the mood for a mug of Mel Horowitz's famous chocolate-overload cocoa?"

Translation: Daddy wants to share details. I smiled, feeling way included. "I'm there—but only if you melt marshmallows on top. And providing you allow me to vent about my night. Which was far, *far* from really great."

Daddy laughed. And over the next hour we traded

stories. Skipping the part about being at Club Metro, I told him about Richard and his name-dropping, condescending attitude. Later it occurred to me that I probably *could* have confessed to the club sidebar. Daddy was so over the moon about Melissa that he probably wouldn't even have freaked.

Daddy had taken her to the Palm, where they'd shared a quiet booth and caught up on all the years they'd been out of touch. Melissa had married the guy she'd dumped Daddy for—Doug Hellinger. In the early years of their marriage, she'd toiled for a small firm, while he'd finished law school. Her story after that was way stereotypical. Once he graduated, he joined a high-profile corporate firm and worked eighty hours a week, racing up the ladder of success. Alas, as the years went by, he and Melissa grew apart, their interests fully diverging. Doug devoted himself to making major bucks for his firm, while Melissa insisted on pro bono work.

Daddy explained, "Melissa feels her law degree is best used to help people who can't afford counsel. She does her share of income-producing cases, but she devotes ten hours a week to a free law clinic."

Okay, so admittedly? When Daddy first walked in the door, I was wary. But as I listened to him talk about her, I couldn't help but be majorly impressed. This Melissa blast-from-the-past had all the markings of a keeper. She sounded as if she had a really good heart. Apparently, she also shared Daddy's love for art, music, and the outdoors. In fact, after dinner, they'd swung by the Getty Center to pick up tickets for a concert. After that they'd gone to the beach.

"The beach! That is so romantic, Daddy!"

He blushed. "We were actually sitting on the dunes, talking. It was so amazing. In spite of the divergent paths our lives took, we have so much in common. That's where we were when you called. And that's how come I had no clue what time it was. I was reminiscing, telling her about your mom, about you, about how proud I am of the way you're turning out."

I wiped the cocoa mustache from my face and glowed. It sounded like Daddy's perfect evening—a favorite restaurant, the beach, talking about me.

It was 4:15 A.M. when I looked at the clock. Drowsiness ruled. I couldn't stifle the yawns anymore. Contentedly, I rose and gave Daddy a peck on the cheek. "I'm glad you had a great date, Daddy, but I'm sacking it. G'night."

I trundled up the steps and was just at the top when Daddy called out, "Oh, by the way, it turns out Melissa and I have something else in common. Something very important. Daughters."

Slowly, I turned around and yawned. "Is that so?"

"It is. And imagine this, Cher—she's your age."

It's not as if every back-to-school day doesn't have its share of crisis, but this turned out to be a Manic Monday for the millennium. Worse, it would lead to full-tilt trauma-rama Tuesday. Like everything that could have gone weird, did.

It started when I dashed out to go to school. No Beverly Hills sunshine to greet me. No smog, either. Instead, it felt tinny. Unwelcoming. An El Niño—

intense rain had fully soaked the driveway, and clouds covered the sky, threatening frizz. It was the kind of day malls were built for. But school beckoned.

Throwing my book-laden backpack into my Jeep, I jumped in and hit the accelerator. Lightly, I thought. Still, I fully skidded off the wet cobblestones, unintentionally trampling a furious flower bed freshly planted by the gardener. Oops, my bad—though not my fault. Not an auspicious beginning to the day.

Fifteen minutes later I pulled into our school's valet parking lot. After picking up my ticket, I bumped into De—solo.

Aiming for jaunty, I was all, "Hey, girlfriend, where's your mustached half?" Normally she and Murray drive to school together. She shrugged. "He bagged, no explanation. Whatever."

She was uncharacteristically silent as we headed off to the Quad. Like if it wasn't for the sound of platforms on concrete, there would have been no sound coming from her at all. "Having issues much, De?"

No answer.

I tried again. "Dionne—hello, this is me. Virtual sister Cher Horowitz. Your t.b. since forever, for forever, through excess poundage, bad hair days, sporadic fashion flaws. You can tell me anything."

De bristled. "There's nothing to tell. I mean, it's just been strange. Murray suddenly morphed from unbearably possessive to uncharacteristically scarce. Since Saturday night, he's beeped me only once.

And that was to say he couldn't pick me up for school."

I frowned. "I bet it's Richard. He probably bruised your boo's already battered ego."

De shrugged. "Could be. At least the golden cousin returned to his exalted life at Stanford as a friend of Chelsea. I'm just glad he's gone."

We hit the cappuccino machine on the way to homeroom. I swiped my credit card and got for both of us. As we walked down the corridor, sipping our light froth decafs, and nodding to all our freshman and sophomore worshippers, I opined, "Murray probably needs you more than ever, De. He's just too upset to even confess. We'll both have to do our bolstering best today."

Okay, so . . . swing and a miss. Or some other sports metaphor. Murray didn't need our ego-repair service. He acted fully self-assured and cool all day. In fact, he acted like the weather—chilly. Toward us, anyway.

But it wasn't Murray's 'tude that tripped my inner alarm. It was Sean's. He seemed jittery. Like he had something to hide, some 411 that made him majorly uncomfortable. When I tried to pry, Sean resisted.

"What's your deal, Sean?" I coaxed when I caught up with him between classes. "How come every time De and I approach, you're like slinking around corners or suddenly have an emergency call to make?"

In response, Sean remembered a dentist's appointment he had to cancel. He whipped out his cellular and dashed away.

Murray's and Sean's bizarre behavior continued all day. Murray displayed zilch interest in De. Not even when she casually mentioned spending lunch hour watching the boys' basketball team practice. In real life, the thought of De in such close proximity to the jock contingent would have sent Murray into the possessive zone. But today? Not even. It was as if he barely heard her. Diagnosis? Murray was withholding. We just had to figure out what.

De refused to obsess. Whatever. She'll call me on an as-needed basis. But when the phone rang later that afternoon, it wasn't my bud, but my pop. Did I remember he was going out with Melissa tonight after work? Could I fend for myself about dinner?

I chuckled. "Duh, Daddy. I'm the champion dinner-fender. Just like I was last night, when you went out with her. It's totally cool. Have a great time."

It really was beyond cool. It's parent manipulation 101: a happy, if slightly guilty, Daddy is a generous Daddy. One who didn't flinch later when I mentioned the flower-bed-flattening episode. And a generous Daddy fully equates to the Cher wing. It's in the bag.

De's distress call didn't come until the next day—lunch period on Tuesday. I was headed to the cafeteria when my cellular rang.

De sounded halting. I couldn't decide if that foretold trauma or triumph. She just wasn't herself.

"Where are you, De?" I scanned the hallway. Our peers clustered around lockers, depositing books before heading for the cafeteria. I focused on De's locker, but she wasn't there. Then I heard a foreign sound. "What's that background noise?"

"Dribbling," she answered. "It's the girls' basketball team dribbling."

Confusion ruled. "You joined?"

De's voice was strained. "I'm in the girls' locker room. Cher—please come. I need you."

My eyes went wide. I panicked. The girls' locker room was our shelter when the crisis was beyond mall troll, when issues were so confidential that being in the bathroom was dicey. But the locker room, after being vacated by all random sports teams—especially during lunch period—afforded total privacy. I stashed my phone in my bag and darted down the hall.

On a lonely bench in row 7 sat De. Her Voyage signature crumpled lingerie dress, which had looked incredibly chic this morning, was tragically merely crumpled now. It matched De's demeanor.

Clutching her books to her chest, she stared into space. I checked her eyes: her makeup remained stellar, so she hadn't been sobbing. I checked her pulse: it was racing. I felt her forehead: no fever, but those little sweat break-out dots had begun to congregate. Diagnosis: De was dazed and confused.

I scoped out the entire locker room and assured her that we were solo. Then I sat down next to her and she spilled it. "Murray . . . told me . . . a little while ago . . . that . . . he needs . . . his space."

"Space? What does that mean . . . exactly?"

De faced me square on. "What does it usually mean when boys say that, Cher? You would know."

Hello, *ouch*. But I let De's harsh slide. I wouldn't hold her responsible for anything she blurted mid-trauma. Besides, I did know what she meant. Translation of "space": "You've been dumped." I have been there. A total of once. But De hasn't. Especially not by Murray. In that relationship, De wears the Capris. She's the dumper—he, the dumpee. Murray is over the moon about De. He's got their entire future planned. It was De who sporadically did the breaking up. And De who decided when the time for making up was ripe.

I put a consoling arm around her, but she shook it off, bristling. "I don't need comforting, Cher. Exactly. I'm just . . . stunned, I guess."

"De," I murmured softly, allowing her to grieve, "it's okay. Tell me what else Murray said."

She drew a deep breath and delivered. Yesterday Murray knew he was going to break up with her, but he didn't have the courage to tell her. So instead, he told Sean. Which accounted for their weirdness all day. Finally, today, between fourth and fifth period, right in the hallway, he managed to spit it out. His reason? In a word: Richard.

"Richard!" I squealed indignantly. "What did he have to do with it?"

De held her chin up. "He made Murray realize that college and his future are coming sooner than he thinks. That he's wasting what should be his carefree high school years stuck with 'the old ball and chain.'"

"And the ball and chain would be . . . ."

"Apparently, me." De spat that last bit out. And that's when her huge hazel eyes welled with pent-up

41

tears. I fished for a tissue and tried to think of some-thing insightful yet compassionate to say.

I'm sure I would have thought of something, but just then the locker room door burst open with such force that it smashed against the wall. We both jumped. I was about to see what the emergency intrusion was, but it announced itself.

Amber. Gasping for breath, she came flying at us. "The-the-there you are!" she sputtered, clutching the spot on her chest where her heart might be—if she had one. Unsurprisingly, she didn't notice De's puffy eyes. Or the fact that we were in deep crisis.

"You call yourself friends! You deserted me in my time of need!" she charged, her chest heaving.

I tried to shoo her away. "Amber, exit. We're hav-ing a moment. And it doesn't concern you. And segue: we never called ourselves your friends. You just assumed."

What Amber heard was "Sit down and share."

She could barely speak. "I—I—I'm not who I think I am!" she finally stammered.

And the reason this qualifies as a crisis would be? Delusion is Amber's middle name. Yet her pro-nouncement did momentarily distract De from her own drama. She dittoed my thoughts. "Like you ever were who you thought you were, Amber? Repeat after me: You never were popular. You never had style. You were never Baldwin-bait. You were never—"

"Amber Marins!" she screeched. "I'm not Amber Marins!"

Okay, so she had our attention. De and I regarded

her quizzically. Before we could say anything, Amber dug into her Gianfranco Ferre tote and hastily withdrew a half-open, pint-size carton of skimmed milk.

"Look! Look at this picture!" she screamed, shoving it in our faces. "This is *me*—the missing child. I'm the face on the milk carton!!"

Chapter 5

*T*he face on the milk carton? As if. The poster child for obsessive-compulsive cosmetic surgery maybe," I retorted. But Amber didn't hear me. She prattled on about her lifestyle-threatening crisis.

Weirdness ruled. I spent the rest of the afternoon in deep crisis control.

"Think before you freak," I counseled De. "Murray will totally come crawling back the nanosecond Richard's residual attitude wears off. And then, girlfriend, you can name the gift. He'll be so contrite, the mall is yours. In fact, I think we should start shopping now."

I couldn't tell if De bought my scenario. Secretly, I planned to collar Sean and get the full dish.

And as for Amber, the face on the milk carton? As if! Well . . . okay, upon closer inspection, the little girl did share Amber's birthday. And she did look frighteningly similar to Original-Nose Amber. De and I had the dubious distinction of knowing her that long.

But hello? Amber stolen? Like in five seconds, any rational thief would return her. Who'd want that life sentence? Talk about prison.

But being returned was Amber's worst nightmare. Convinced that she was the face on the milk carton, she spent the rest of the day ranting about how she refused to be found. Her life now is the pinnacle of perfection—and only bound to get better. What if her original parents took her back? What if they were unwealthy? It was unthinkable. Way *sacré coeur!*

Between De's traumatic shock and Amber's mock trauma, the day spiraled downhill faster than Kevin Costner's career.

Which left uphill as the only direction for the rest of the week.

Grievously, not even. As the week progressed, the situation regressed. I did a double take when I saw Murray in homeroom the next day. The dude formerly known as manic Murray was subdued. His hue du jour was brown. Navy the next day. Black on Friday. Nary a swatch of citrus. It wasn't heinous; it just wasn't him.

Not that I could remark on his quick-change image switch. He assiduously avoided eye contact with De and by extension me.

De's reaction was predictable. I mean, if you know her. She went profoundly proud, affecting a "You dumped me? As if!" attitude toward Murray. In PE, within earshot of all senior girls, she asserted that *she'd* been thinking of breaking up with him. No one does persuasion like De. When I looked around, it was clear that she had fully convinced most of our peer group. Except for one peer who begged to differ: me.

And then there was Amber, whose need to find other outlets had reached epic proportions. She was now fully obsessed about being the milk carton girl. And Amber could give Calvin Klein obsession lessons. It became her theme, informing every aspect of her life. Her mission? "Under no circumstances will my real parents find me!"

She changed her phone number to an unlisted one. Which seemed all "Why bother?" since like who ever calls her anyway? She proclaimed every day Halloween, by wearing disguises to school. One day she wrapped herself from head to toe in white tulle, her version of a third world woman. Another day it was dark shades, blond wig shrouded in a scarf, and high-collared turtleneck.

Which was all a mega "Why bother?" Who knew her insane costumes and wigs were supposed to mean she was incognito? If anything, Amber managed to look more herself than ever.

Whatever. While I pride myself on being the first facilitator of friends in need, how could I take Amber's quasi-crisis seriously? It paled profoundly next to the De-Murray wound.

I tried to collar Sean, but that was as useless as cash in the Beverly Center. And segue: If Sean was bummed about the breakup of ostensibly his two best friends, he wasn't showing it. Sunny-side-up Sean not only saw the bright side of the sitch, he exploited it.

When I finally got him to interface, during chemistry class, he explained, "I feel for De and all, but Murray's new situation works for me. Now me and my man can double-date."

I rolled my eyes. "Sean, there was nothing preventing you from double-dating with De and Murray. What's different now?"

This time he rolled his eyes. "Everything, Cher. Now we'll both be on first dates together. It won't be me all awkward with the ladies and him all smooth with his steady anymore. It's a level playing field."

Logic takes a holiday.

The gruesome twosome wasted no time plunging into the Bronson Alcott dating pool. By Thursday they'd asked out the two Tiffanys. I tried to be "Whatever," but inwardly? I was fully wiggin'. Dating two of our friends was so in De's face. Of course, had De not announced her plans to break up with Murray, Tiffany would never have accepted the date. It's like that famous slogan "Friends don't let friends date other friends' boyfriends." Or something.

I had to do some serious soul-searching. But it was eighth period and I had PE, so I had to put up with the grievous annoyance of dodgeballs aimed at my shins. Hello, have we learned nothing from the Tonya Harding/Nancy Kerrigan knee encounter?

Still, by the time the bell rang, I realized what my

part was in all this. I would not intervene. I would allow nature to take its course. And until such time as Murray came crawling back to De? The shingle outside my door was Dr. "Solidarity & Support" Horowitz. De and I would self-actualize. We'd go into full Shop Therapy and upgrade everything: our wardrobes, our social lives, our inner Bettys, our personal space. I silently resolved to involve De in my plans for the Cher wing.

In a weird way, it kind of worked that De needed me. Lately, Daddy didn't. He was out with Melissa every night.

Except for Sunday. That's when, during brunch, he announced he wasn't going out with her that night. She was coming here.

"I want you to meet her," Daddy said casually over egg whites and pulp-enriched orange juice. "So I thought we'd all have dinner together. Tonight."

I tried to hide my surprise and match his casual attitude. "Uh, sure. Bumpin' idea, Daddy. It's kind of late notice, but I think I could get a reservation at Wolfgang Puck's Café. Or, if they're booked solid, maybe Obachine." I was going through my mental restaurant index, which is probably why I didn't hear Daddy the first time.

"Do you think you could get a reservation someplace closer to home?" He had a distinctly bemused tone.

"Closer? You mean Barney Greengrass? I agree, the terrace overlooking *tout* 90210 is trendy, but it's primarily a brunch scene—"

He interrupted. "What about Casa Horowitz? I hear the scene there is pretty neat. And there's spectacular people-watching to be had."

I assumed Daddy was joking, but his periwinkle blues were all, not even.

I drew a breath and considered. Short declarative phrases came out. "You want. To invite Melissa. To dinner. At our house. Tonight."

"Not just her," Daddy said, getting up from the table and clearing our dishes. "Tara, too."

"Who's Tara?"

"Her daughter," Daddy reminded me. "I told you about her, Cher."

He had, but I'd conveniently forgotten. It's not as if there was an actual *reason* to think about her. Until now.

"Don't you think it's a little soon?" My bad. The words tumbled out by themselves.

Daddy's look said, "Don't go there, Cher." Yet I stumbled on. "I mean . . . you barely know her." Open mouth, insert foot.

But instead of being bugged, Daddy softened. "I know her twenty-five years, Cher. On what planet does that constitute 'barely'?"

Chastised, I backpedaled furiously. "Well, duh, you know that's not what I meant. I meant . . ." But he'd already turned his back and, platter-laden, headed toward the kitchen.

I tried to Band-Aid. "You're right, Daddy. It's a stellar idea. We'll eat here. I'll order in from—"

Daddy stopped and shot me an over-the-shoulder grin. "No need to order in, sweetheart.

I'm going to barbecue. It's supposed to be a beautiful night, and our grill could use the action. It never gets used. Melissa's bringing the side dishes. It'll be fun."

Side dishes? Fun? Barbecue? That is so *King of the Hill*.

A mental picture formed. Daddy with tongs? Leaning over a grill, with one of those heinous slogan-laden aprons that say, Kiss the Cook. Or Born 2 BBQ? Using sitcom-dad expressions, like "Come and get it!" And "Who wants a burned one?" Handing out grilled turkey dogs and barbecued chicken to Melissa and her my-age daughter? The picture was massively surreal—hello, Dali.

And excuse me, when exactly did I pass the signs that say "You are now leaving Beverly Hills" and "Entering Brady Bunch land"?

What I needed was mulling-over time with my main. I hit speed dial on my phone, but tragically, De wasn't home. Her voice mail airily informed anyone who called—clearly, she hoped Murray—that she was out. On a date. "With Jed, the captain of the basketball team." Yesterday's message had been, "With Jamie, from UCLA." The night before, she'd boasted, "With Philippe, the studmuffin soccer dude model on the Abercrombie and Fitch bags."

Okay, like mea partly culpa. Had I not encouraged De to upgrade her social life? And any girl with a pulse would bow to her success in scoring a date with the hot A & F dude!

But a little voice in my head was all, "Serial dating? That is so Winona Ryder." But the louder voice in my head drowned out everything. It was all, "Daddy's bringing Melissa home! She's bringing side dishes! And her daughter! For a nuclear-family-esque Sunday cookout!"

Never had Daddy done something so extreme.

My life was suddenly all warp speed. I took several deep breaths and over my homework, without benefit of t.b. input, self-mulled.

Somewhere between trig, English lit, and the Neiman's catalog, I found a higher truth: I'm going to have to let go sometime. It's Daddy's life. Learning from his mistakes is a growth experience. My role is to accept, support, and act out that famous cliché "If it makes him happy, I can deal."

But could I? Duh. Like that deeply spiritual advertising poem, "I can."

So after I finished my homework—which included a killer essay on Supreme Court decisions—I put on a cute little Rancho Hot Springs promotional terry-cloth sun visor and went out back to survey. Even on short notice, I could do barbecue chic.

Our backyard is fully standard. Our ceramic-tile-lined, kidney-shaped pool is usefully surrounded by a chaise-longue obsessed mahogany patio deck. Accessories include several tempered glass tables, an awning-covered swing for two, and a ropy hammock that no one ever uses. A half acre beyond is where our tennis courts live. Off to the right, our herb garden of earthly delights, and to the left, our neighbor's house. Land in Beverly Hills is majorly premium.

The whole scene is bodaciously bucolic, dotted

with pricey marble sculptures and one excellent Evian-spewing fountain. It's all maintained and lovingly cared for by a team of designer-quality landscape artists. And this season, a totally tawny pool boy named Warren. Or Darren. Potentially Orrin. Articulation is so not his strong suit—looking hot in bathing suits is.

Any of the above staff would have known where the barbecue grill was, but grievously, since it was Sunday, they were all off. Daddy had gone to our local gourmet supermarket to pick up what he cornily called "all the fixin's"—steaks, burgers, buns, chicken, and Charcoal Companion.

Ergo, the task of finding the grill was mine. I've never personally seen it, but Daddy insisted we had one. It had to be in the environs. I paced the area directly behind the pool and off toward our neighbors. No grill.

Finally, after an extensive search, I found it. It was draped in a black cover-up, so I assumed it was one of our sculptures, under wraps for repair. But when I lifted the cover to double-check, there it was—Weber: the finest name in grills. A cache of ornaments—later Daddy explained they were outdoor cooking utensils—hung from the side.

Serendipitously, it was on wheels, which made lugging it closer to the pool area doable. After finishing that labor-intense task, I occupied myself with happier things: decorating. I found Chinese lanterns in our storage closet and strung them up. I dotted the area with aromatherapy and bug-repellent candles. I did whimsical straw place mats instead of a tablecloth and opted for everyday stainless instead of sterling.

Then I went to the china closet and dug out our Orrefors crystal stemware and matching ice bucket. I used Amalfi Mediterranean china. When I was done, I surveyed. The eclectic mix of down-home barbecue and upmarket accessories was stellar. Besides, you could take the clambake theme only so far.

When Daddy returned, he was majorly proud of the job I'd done. Mentioning that he expected Melissa and her daughter at five o'clock, he decided to get to work doing something called marinating. I deduced it was cooking terminology. Has Daddy been clandestinely watching the Cooking Channel? What's *that* about?

I decided to get to my work: dressing. I went straight for my computer, into which all my ensembles are uploaded. There was an Appropriate Ensembles file for Meeting Daddy's Date, but there was none for "What to Wear When Daddy Brings His Date Home." I'd have to do some mix and matching on my own. Eventually, I opted to go straight barbecue. White Prada Capri pants, platform slides, crisp white shirt worn collar up and tied at the waist—totally Sharon Stone at the Oscars. I traded my sun visor for a floppy Joan & David's cloche. When I finished, I pirouetted in front of my free-standing oval mirror. The statement said, "Jaunty, not jaded; casual chic, not backyard hick." Stellar!

And just in time. The readout on my bedside digital indicated 5:00 P.M. The time was here—but Melissa and her side dishes were not. Nor had they shown by 5:20 or 5:30, considered more acceptable than actual on-time. Strike one, I thought, then immediately slapped my wrist. "Bad Cher. Those who live in tardy houses shall not throw stones."

But by six, when they still hadn't appeared, I began to fret—for Daddy's sake. What if they'd stood him up? He'd be crushed! I looked out my backyard window, where I spied him bent over the grill, with a paintbrush-like cooking tool. My worst fears were confirmed. He was all Daddy domestic, humming a happy tune, wearing a tall white Dr. Seuss chef's hat, and an apron with the slogan Born 2 BBQ.

In spite of myself, I had to smile. Grown-ups can be so precious when they're out of character. I bounced downstairs and went outside to join him.

Daddy looked up when he heard me. "Hey, Pumpkin, don't you look smart!"

"Hey yourself," I responded, pointing at his chapeau. "You, on the other hand, look decidedly unlawyerly."

Daddy tilted his head and laughed. "Exactly what I was going for. There's more to life than work, you know."

I scrunched my nose. "What time was our company supposed to debut?"

Daddy checked his watch and looked up, surprised. His expression swiftly changed to concerned. "It's six already? They should have been here an hour ago. I hope nothing's wrong. I'd better go call."

He put down his brush and took a step toward the house. But just then the front doorbell rang. It had to be them. I dashed to answer it—but stopped in my tracks for a quick style-check soundbite. "Lose the chef's hat, Daddy."

At Daddy's confused look, I reminded him, "Melissa's daughter has never been here or spent quality time with you—"

"And she might decide I'm some corny old geezer, huh?" Daddy laughed, but he knows I rule in matters of style and took my advice. He was on my heels as I flung open the front door.

The minute I saw them, I fully gasped.

It was déjà view—all over again.

Chapter 6

Okay, so that First Impressionist thing—that you never have a second chance to make one? Melissa didn't need a do-over. Her debut was ragin'. Decked out in cocoa Ann Taylor linen pants and cardigan set, accessorized with a barbecue-appropriate see-through food tote, she seemed sensitive, yet consequential. Melissa wore her honey brown hair tucked neatly behind her ears, which sported classic stud earrings. Her makeup accented her long-lashed cocoa eyes and smooth skin. The survey said? A woman who knows her hues and her moisturizer.

Melissa's most furious feature, though, was her smile. It was such the warm, natural, you-can-tell-me-anything beam. As aimed at Daddy, it spoke encyclopedic volumes.

The girl who lagged a few steps behind her was also carrying one of those see-through, snap-lid food containers. She didn't need a second chance to make a first impression, either. But that's because she'd already made one two weekends ago.

Before I could stop myself, I blurted, "Gwen!"

Hello, it was totally her. The smoke-in-my-face tough chick from Club Metro. Only without the random tails, bridge-of-her-nose dot, or camouflage drawstrings. Today she was in straight-leg luster pants, sleeveless tank, and silver Skecher high-tops.

Melissa whirled around, confused, as Daddy urged, "Come in, come in. We'll make the introductions inside."

They stepped into our domed, checked marble-tiled foyer and looked around. They were majorly impressed. But who wouldn't be?

"Cher, I'd like you to meet Melissa Hellinger. Melissa, this is my daughter, Cher," Daddy was saying.

To her gold-card credit, she neither engulfed me in faux affection, nor did the I've-heard-so-much-about-you cliché. She flashed a deep dental display and offered her hand. "I'm thrilled to meet you, Cher. Thank you for inviting us."

Snaps for her. Deftly, she acknowledged that Daddy and I were a team. If he'd invited her, it meant I had, too.

Then she slipped her arm around her daughter's waist. "And this is Tara."

Whatever. Like a thorny rose by any other name and minus the heinous dot, it was still totally her. As I took a tentative step forward to shake her hand, I peered into her catlike, alert green eyes. She knew it was me. Yet neither of us said a word beyond "Hi."

There was no point in Daddy knowing I'd been to Club Metro. And I had a sneaking suspicion Melissa had no knowledge of Gwen's—that is, Tara's—whereabouts two weeks ago, either.

Daddy, who'd keenly observed our first interface, chuckled. "Do you two know each other?"

Silence.

"You looked . . . like someone else," I finally sputtered.

"I get that all the time." Her tone was way caustic. More than the moment called for.

I was about to say something to cover up the awkwardness when Tara did it for me. She shoved her Tupperware tote at her mom, flipped around, and dripped sarcastic. "Is there a bathroom on this floor of the mansion?"

"Follow me," I responded, ignoring her derision. But as I led the way to the powder room, I intuited why she needed it: she was going to light up. Casually, I mentioned, "The smoke alarm is in the hallway right outside the bathroom. It's very sensitive."

She didn't answer me.

When I returned, Daddy and Melissa were still in the foyer. She was giving her tardy excuse: Tara didn't want to come.

"We argued for an hour," Melissa lamented. "She insisted she had nothing to wear. Then she refused to dry her hair. It was such a struggle! I don't know what's gotten into her. She's never like this."

Daddy went wise and empathetic. "Relax. It's perfectly natural for her to be resistant. Just give me and Cher time. We'll win her over."

Okay, so when did winning her over end up on *my* to-do list? Adjunct: when Tara emerged a few minutes later, rolling a breath cover-up Mentos on her tongue—to mock me—I didn't want her on any list. Daddy had no idea what he was in for. Guilelessly, he invited everyone outside.

Tara hissed under her breath as she followed me out, "Oooh, let the weenie roast begin."

Hello! She'd just insulted Daddy's efforts to make a good impression. I spun around, about to rag on her, but I stopped myself just in time. I pride myself on being more evolved than that. Instead, I went faux empathetic. "I totally relate. How lame is a barbecue? But, you know, the 'rents think it's righteous. We might as well make the best of it."

In response, Tara rolled her eyes and brushed past me. I was left standing there, holding the sliding door open.

Melissa was genuinely charmed by the effort I'd put into decorating. "The lanterns! And the candles! Oh, and look at those place mats—aren't they cute! Cher, this was so sweet of you."

Daddy beamed. "That's my girl. She did it all by herself. In no time she turned our backyard into a perfect setting for a Sunday barbecue."

Modestly, I demurred. "Tscha! A few accessories sprinkled here and there. You can never go wrong. It's one of the rules I live by."

Sensing Tara's exclusion, Daddy turned to her. "Your mom tells me you're the best brownie baker in the county—can't wait to taste the batch you brought."

So that was Tara's culinary contribution. Instantly, I flashed on that fairy tale, *Arsenic and Old Lace*. What if Tara tried to poison us with an unspecific bacterium? I shuddered.

Tara didn't acknowledge Daddy's compliment. Instead, she yawned rudely and plopped onto one of the chaise longues. "What's to drink?"

"Glad you asked," Daddy cheerily responded, motioning to the table where I'd displayed a stellar selection of designer water, power juices, and trendy iced teas. "What's your pleasure, Tara?"

Somehow, I knew the words "My pleasure is being anywhere but here" were about to leave her lips, so I jumped up, loudly exclaiming, "Music! We need music!" I flipped the switch that pipes music to the backyard. Celine Dion's power-whining about "Muh heart weel go o-o-o-on" served a useful purpose: Tara's obnoxious response was drowned out.

The comfort level during dinner ebbed and tided. Or something. Over burgers, kabobs and those fixin's—which turned out to be culinary accessories—major stuff emerged. Point A: Cookout food can be edible. Maybe it was the Charcoal Companion, but Daddy's kabobs had potential. Point B: Melissa is such the quality Betty, fully right for Daddy. Point C: He totally gets it.

I mean, could it have been more kickin', the way they stood side by side at the grill, talking, laughing, flipping turkey burgers? They were so connecting.

Tara, who—bad Cher—I had begun to think of as Melissa's evil spawn, continued to sulk. Stretched out on the chaise, morosely sipping an iced tea, she personified that *Good Will Hunting* theme, "Miss Misery."

During the sit-down portion of dinner, Daddy kept offering her stuff—"Would you like a turkey burger?" Or, "How 'bout a kabob?" He even uttered the words from my surrealistic dream, "Who wants a burned one?"

But she was all, "I'm not hungry." The only thing she ate was her mom's side dish, killer three-alarm chili.

Taking a cue from Daddy, Melissa tried to maintain a cheery exterior, but Tara's moodiness was clearly wearing her down. Yet, instead of scolding her daughter—which would have been egregiously embarrassing—gamely, she kept the conversation light. She asked me the standard questions.

"What are you taking at school, Cher?"

I ran down my list of majors and electives. Melissa was impressed, especially when I noted some of the cutting-edge options at Bronson Alcott. Like Asian languages to better communicate with our growing multi-culti population.

Melissa noted, "They don't offer Chinese at Tara's school. I bet you'd take it if they did, right, honey?"

Tara snorted. "You'd lose."

Melissa's expression was pained, but she shifted smoothly back to casual. "You know, one of my current cases, a custody battle, reminds me of that. A woman I represent is fighting to keep her daughter at home with her—in the house she grew up in—but the district her ex lives in has a better school system. That's his argument, anyway, for the daughter moving in with him."

Helpfully, I suggested, "Why not just pay for the school in the dad's district and allow the daughter to live at home with her mom?"

Tara rolled her eyes. "Because money solves everything. Right, Cher?"

I considered. "No, not everything. But in this case, it could enable win-win."

Tara retorted, "How about letting the kid decide what she wants to do? Or, how's *this* for a revolutionary concept? Her parents find a way to get along." She stared at her mom. Mission accomplished: Melissa turned red.

Awkward moment alert! Attempted save by Daddy, who blurted, "You know what, I've got an idea. We're just about finished. Cher, why not show Tara your room? That'll give Melissa and me a chance to clean up. Then we'll all have dessert."

Show Tara my room? That is so third grade! I started to protest, but one look at Daddy and I realized—lock my lips and throw away the key. A calming moment between him and Melissa was called for.

Because Daddy needed me, I aided and abetted. Fully reluctantly.

Surprisingly, Miss Misery didn't protest but followed me into the house. Which created the first two-of-us-alone moment. For Daddy's sake, I aimed for friendliness. "I'm really glad you could come. I mean, the invite was on such short notice."

Tara crabbed, "Like I had a choice. I wasn't invited. I was subpoenaed."

The urge to blurt "You're dismissed!" was overwhelming. But I fought it. Instead, I swiftly searched for another topic. When in doubt? Fashion is the answer. "Kickin' luster pants," I commented keenly. "Where'd you get them?"

"What's it to you? Like we might shop in the same—"

Tara abruptly stopped in her tracks and gasped. She seemed stunned by the entryway to my room: white wood-frame double doors inset with stained-glass panels of lilies and gladiolas. She ran her finger along a lily.

"Wow" was all she could muster.

I invited her in. She scanned the terrain, her eyes darting from the poufy pink draperies, to the pink striped wallpaper, queen-size bed, faux marble desk, divan, mood-lighting fireplace, and freestanding oval mirror. After her reaction to my doors, I naively assumed she'd softened. At least, I expected a compliment. Not even. Instead, she went snide.

"So this is what Daddy's money buys you. Welcome to the dollhouse."

I fully bristled. "Excuse me, Tara. I don't see you being deprived. Your mom is an attorney, after all."

She turned on her heel and stared at me. "Not that I owe you an explanation, but for one thing, as you may know, she does a lot of pro bono work. Which means—"

"Hello! I know what it means. It means she fights

63

for people who can't afford pricey attorneys. I fully salute her, Tara."

"Well, salute this, Cher. I couldn't care less about the money. But going through a no-fault divorce changed a lot of things in our house. And besides, even if I could afford a royal palace, I would never prissy it up like this."

I took major offense—who was she to diss my decor? But again, I aimed for equanimity. "Really? And just what would you do, Tara? I'm open to decorating advice."

Tara suddenly turned and leaped up onto my bed, where she began bouncing up and down. "For starters, I'd lose the girly-girl wallpaper and change this from Barbie's playhouse to the appearance of a room where an actual thinking, breathing, nonsuperficial human lives."

I was starting to steam, but I let her finish. "And you would accomplish that by? . . ."

"Trash and burn, Cher. I'd rip up everything and paint the entire room black, including the ceiling, and—"

I was stunned. "Black! As if! Excuse me, I think I know my hues, and while *noir* is a formidable shade for a little black dress, shrouding an entire room in it is beyond dreary. I shudder to imagine living in—" I sputtered, picturing my cheery personal space as imagined by Darth Vader.

Tara ignored me. "I'd stick those glow-in-the-dark stars up on the ceiling."

I'd seen that look, in a college dorm. It was beyond cheesy.

"I bet there's one thing you wouldn't change," I said. "Follow me."

I led Tara to the alcove that abuts my room and through which my closet lives. As she watched, I hit the remote. My full couture collection paraded before us. Then I switched on the computer and demonstrated how ensembles get put together.

That had to impress her. But not even. She was all, "Oooh, a mechanized, computer-operated closet. Cher Horowitz, you've got nothing on Ivanka."

Finally, I'd had enough. I turned off the computer and folded my arms.

"Look, Tara. I propose we drop the charade now. We both know we've met before. Under less than stellar circumstances."

She shifted and shrugged. "So?"

Her nonchalance unnerved me, so I went with the fully lame "Does your mother know you hang out smoking in the girls' room at Club Metro?"

"Pul-eeze, Goody Two-shoes. Ooops, make that"— she pointed to the shoe-obsessed shelves that line my alcove—"goody *two hundred* shoes. What my mother doesn't know won't hurt her. And for that matter, does Daddy Do-Right know where *you* were that night?"

I huffed, "Excuse me, that was different. I was there only under duress. To support a friend."

"Right. Whatever."

Tara, feigning boredom, strode over to the window that overlooks our backyard. She peered out and remarked, "Speaking of charades, the little one being played out by your father and my mother isn't very original. Throwing us together, trying to get us to be friends. Like that would ever happen. They just wanted to ditch us so they could be alone together. Look."

Over her shoulder, I peeked outside. Daddy and Melissa were sitting on the outdoor swing. His arm was around her shoulder, he was comforting her. The scene was totally tender. It reminded me of what I was supposed to be doing: winning over Tara.

"Okay, look, just because we started off on the wrong foot doesn't mean we can't be . . . at some point . . . down the road . . . friends." I hoped she didn't notice my totally tentative tone.

Tara turned away from the window, snickering. "Actually, Cher? Meeting at Club Metro? I think we started out on the right foot. At least it was honest, an unforced encounter."

While I disagreed about the footing, in a weird way she was right.

Tara added, "That reminds me. You might want to turn the smoke alarm back on outside the downstairs bathroom."

I was aghast. She'd had the nerve to turn it off and put us at unnecessary risk? I started to shake my finger at her and deliver a diatribe about selfishness.

But Tara rudely whisked past me to the other side of the room. She pushed back the curtains of the floor-to-ceiling windows and peered outside. Matter-of-factly, she said, "I think you have a stalker."

Chapter 7

What!"

I rushed over, threw open the window, and stuck my head outside. I didn't see anything at first. Then I focused on the manicured shrubbery that lines our driveway. Tara was right. Sort of. There was someone—some*thing*—out there.

Swathed in purple padding, it resembled a runaway baby Ewok. I yelled down. "Looking for your home planet, Amber?"

Forefinger to her lips, she snapped back, "Don't call me that!"

While I could think of a thousand other things to call her—TInky-Winky came to mind—I shut the window and dashed downstairs to let her in. Amber's costume was no mirage. She really *was* head-to-toe in purple fleece. And since this *is* Beverly Hills, she was sweating profusely. "I don't think anyone followed me," she gasped. "I'm going upstairs. Put the alarm on."

Amber galloped up the steps two at a time. I rushed after her, trying to figure out a way to explain her and her psychosis to Tara. And vice versa. Amber darted into my room and tried to lock the door. Breathing hard, she yanked off her head-piece and collapsed on my divan. Her hair, bathed in sweat, stuck to her face. It was actually an improvement.

Tara took in the entire scene, fully bemused.

Personally, I was bemused-challenged. But I couldn't help getting in a dig about her costume. "How many Teletubbies had to die for that outfit, Amber?"

Tara giggled—the first smile she'd cracked all evening. Amber serves a worthwhile purpose at last. Quickly, I dispensed with the intros and then commanded the fuzzy-wuzzy psychotic to debrief. "And this better be good," I warned her.

She whined, "Excuse me, I just made a daring escape. Undercover agents were at my door. They came for me!"

I rolled my eyes. "Try again. In the real world."

Tara made herself comfortable on my bed. Too comfortable. She wrapped her arms around one of my overstuffed pillows, clutched it to her, and piped up, "I, for one, am all ears. This sounds good."

Amber didn't need further encouragement. She croaked, "This couple. Out of nowhere, they appeared at my house. They send them as couples, to throw you off. But they can't fool me."

In spite of myself, I asked, "This couple. They claimed to be . . ."

Amber sniffed. "Friends of my parents from out of town. As if!"

Tara said, "But your parents didn't know them?"

"Well, they did . . . that is, they pretended they did." She turned to me for affirmation. "Cher, you know my parents. Appearances are everything. How would it look if they didn't know people who said they knew them? So they invited them in. The enemy!"

"Amber, you are fully deranged," I concluded.

She bolted upright on the divan. "Am I? Then why, after a few hours, did they ask—oh so casually!—to see my baby album?"

Tara was getting into it. She guessed, "Did they, by any chance, whip out pictures of their own brood?"

Amber made a face at Tara. "Excuse me, ruse alert! Of course they did."

"Hello, Amber, comparing embarrassing photos of us before we were fashionable is one of our parents' great joys," I said. "Which, duh, only proves they're exactly who they said—friends. Case closed. You can go home now."

Amber whined, "How could I expect you to understand? If you haven't walked a mile in my stilettos you can't possibly know what I'm going through." After a crocodile sob, she added, "I wasn't about to wait around. I grabbed a disguise and left. I slipped out, undetected. I'm pretty sure they didn't get a good look at the real me."

"Even your mirror hasn't had a good look at the real you in years," I noted.

She ignored me and continued to describe her "daring" escape. "I had to think fast. My usual suite at the Peninsula Hotel was out of the question—that's the first place they'd look. Then they'd track the car. So I forfeited both and ran all the way here. A place my parents wouldn't think to call."

I looped Tara in. "Welcome to Amber-land. She thinks she's the face on the milk carton—a missing child."

Tara arched her eyebrows. "You think you were kidnapped when you were younger? Do you have any memories of living with another family?"

Amber retorted, "Have you never heard of repressed memory syndrome? But that child was me."

I thought Tara might be shocked, but not even. She stretched out on my bed and yawned. "Use my mother. She's a lawyer. Missing children are what she does. She'll dig up the truth."

Before I could react, the intercom lit up. I switched it on. Daddy's voice wafted through. "Cher? Tara? You girls ready for dessert? It's on the table."

"We'll be right down, Daddy."

Reluctantly, I invited Amber to join us, but the drama queen waved me off. "You two kiddies join your biological parents. I need a shower. Cher, I assume acceptable moisturizing soap and other necessities are stocked in the boudoir? Including a guest robe?"

"I'm sure you'll find the facilities amenable. Knock yourself out, Amber."

*　*　*

Dessert, which went without incident, featured Tara's homemade brownies. Poisoned or not, I had to salute their bodacious yumminess.

Our guests left soon after. The door had barely closed when Daddy solicited my opinion. It meant a lot to him. "Be honest, sweetheart. What do you think of Melissa?"

I gave her a total thumbs-up. "She's a full-out righteous Betty, Daddy. And she's over the moon about you. Grievously, she's stuck with Obnoxious Spice for a daughter."

Amazingly, Tara's rampantly rude 'tude hadn't bummed Daddy out. "Tara just needs time to adjust to her mother going out again, that's all."

I frowned. "Not even, Daddy. Angst is so early nineties Seattle. Even Pearl Jam coexists with Ticketmaster now. I mean, hel*lo!*"

Daddy looked confused, but gave me a peck on the cheek. "Give her a chance, Cher."

To do what? Burn the house down? I thought about telling Daddy how Tara had had a cigarette in the bathroom and, worse, turned off the smoke alarm. But something about his dreamy, faraway look stopped me. Unlike Tara, I couldn't bring myself to ruin the moment.

Tragically, when I got back upstairs, Amber had made herself at home. She'd gone into my closet and selected my virgin Dolce & Gabbana outfit! Worse, she was strutting around in my mules, fully vogueing in front of my mirror. Did she even thank me for my hospitality? As if!

Instead, she sighed. "I see *someone* didn't make it to the Paris fashion shows this year. Or the year before." Then she tied a JennaWear geometric scarf around her shoulders and whined, "I'll have to make do with this."

I ignored her disparaging comments. "Amber, lose the drama. You are not a missing child. You have lived close enough to spy on us for our whole lives. I would know if you were stolen. Daddy would know."

She turned on her—hello, *my*—heel. "Really, Cher? You can't even see what's going on in your *own* home. How can you pretend to know what went on in mine so many years ago?"

Sighing, I rearranged the pillows Tara had messed up. "Translation?"

Quoting that famous poem, "I overheard. I deduced. I leaped to dunder-headed conclusions," Amber explained that she'd switched on the intercom in my room and heard every word of my conversation with Daddy.

I was stunned. "Stealing my clothes is one thing, but eavesdropping? The chutzpah level is off the chart, Amber. Even for you."

"Excuse me," she said, strutting back to the mirror. "Desperate times call for desperate measures. I cite: moi in *your* pathetic clothes! But I am the one being stalked. I cannot afford to be oblivious to anything going on around me. Consider yourself lucky, Cher. You may be too blind to see, but I know what's happening here."

"What are you babbling about?" I said, ripping the scarf off her shoulders. "That doesn't go with that."

"I speak of Tara, the object of your disdain. It isn't just her angsty attitude that ruffles your feathers. It's the subtext."

I groaned. "The subtext. On which you, of course, are such the expert."

Amber eased onto the divan, slipped out of my mules, and began to massage her toes. "Tara threatens you—and somewhere under that discount-diva makeup, you know I'm right. Mark my words, Tara is moving in."

"Swing and a miss, Amber. Our parents, fully consenting adults, have been dating for two weeks. In what language does that translate to Tara moving in?"

"Two weekends . . . or every day for two full weeks?" She arched her eyebrows, recently shaped by Anastasia Soare, eyebrow plucker to the stars. "Don't bother doing the math, Cher. I already have. They've gone on a total of fifteen dates. They're ready to take the next step—right through your beautifully etched, stained glass double doors. Bet on it."

I was fuming. "The only bet I'm making is on how long before they commit you, Ambu-lunatic."

Amber took a deep breath and shook her head. "Cher, Cher . . . in your sheltered little world, you are so naïve. I know an interloper when I see one."

I felt a choking sensation. "You've lost it, Amber. I'm driving you home."

Over Amber's protests, I did just that. She slumped down in the car so no one could see her, and agreed to get out only after I assured her that there were no cars in the driveway that didn't belong to her family. The "undercover agents" had left.

I so needed to share the details of Barbecue Sunday with De, but grievously, by the time I went to bed, she still wasn't back from her date. At school the next day, I waited for her in the Quad before homeroom. As soon as I saw her, I rushed up and delivered the detailed dish.

About Tara being the tough chick from the Club Metro bathroom. The one De almost went medieval on!

About Daddy and Melissa.

About Amber being a stalker Teletubby.

And about Amber's rampantly ridiculous theory on Tara—chuh!—moving in.

I had so much to spill, it took a while to realize that De hadn't responded. To anything.

"Knock, knock, De. Anybody home? Don't you find it beyond coincidental that Tara turns out to be—"

De stopped me. "I heard. I'm duly nauseous for you. Puff Girly is Daddy's girlfriend's evil spawn. But you know what? I'm not inhabiting that mental landscape. I am over everything related to Murray. And the memory of being there with him. And his nasty cousin Richard. It's ancient history."

I paused and took a good look at my main. At first, I couldn't figure out what was off about her. Then I realized: her hair. Pinned up haphazardly, it was furiously uncouth. De's aim at an up-do tragically resulted in an up-don't. Guilt engulfed me. I'd been so involved with my own trauma, I hadn't noticed hers. Sympathetically, I commented, "Bad hair day, huh? I feel your pain. It can obscure everything. Are we doing Salon Laurent at lunch?"

De tossed her head back and scoffed, "Hello, it's the new style. Halle Berry at the Oscars. Unswept and unkept."

Not even. It was a frantic cry for help.

I was about to remark on that when her cellular rang. Listening to her end of the conversation, I deduced it was her date du jour. She giggled girlishly. "That's so sweet of you. Uh-huh. I feel the same way. Thursday?" She paused, scanned the Quad, and then said, "I'll be there."

"College boy—Jamie?" I guessed when she clicked off.

De scrunched her nose. "Yesterday's news. No, that was Diego, he's an actor. He just auditioned for *Party of Five*. I met him driving along La Cienega. We both stopped for a red and checked each other out. You know. Anyway, we were just firming up plans for Thursday night."

"De . . ." I paused. How could I put this? I didn't want to hurt her, especially now, in her time of vulnerability. But hello, if I didn't say something—who would? What are virtual sisters for? I went for it.

"Are you sure you want to do this? I mean, so many different boys. Don't take this the wrong way, but is it possible you're overcompensating for lack of Murray?"

Oops, my bad. Timing that is. Just then Murray and Sean ambled by—arms draped around the two Tiffanys. The soresome foursome were massively

75

engaged in animated conversation. Only I saw Murray sheepishly check De from the corner of his eye.

De bristled. "Lack of Murray is liberating. I'm making up for lost time. But"—she paused—"I do have one slight snag. Excess boyage. I sort of accidentally agreed to see Diego and Philippe on Thursday night. Could you pinch-hit? We could double date. Like some other best friends are doing." She nodded in Murray and Sean's direction.

My first reaction was, not even. Random dates are so not the way. Especially when it's just to keep pace with your ex. I needed to channel De's excess energy in a more positive direction. But how? Then it came to me. I remembered our recently scuttled plans for a girl-bonding sleep-over. Impulsively, I suggested a reschedule—for this weekend.

A stunned look came over De's face. "Reschedule? You mean, re-invite everyone to your house? Including, hello, *Tiffany?*"

"Amendment, De: just you and me. We'll do a full beauty blitz, hair and makeup sessions, manicures, pedicures. We'll rent chick flicks. We'll bring in veggie 'za from Spago, BH. We'll gorge. We'll giggle. We'll wax."

De tilted her head, calculating. "Agreed . . ."

I went to high-five her, but she wasn't finished.

". . . If you double date with me."

Okay, so in the end? I wasn't even bummed about that deal. Casa Horowitz had been egregiously empty lately. In a rerun of last week, Daddy was out with Melissa daily. And when he did get in, all he talked about was her. And, postscript: Tara. The evil spawn was causing them both major aggro. I could understand Melissa's agony, but Daddy was empathy overload.

"Tara's grades are slipping. She used to be a top student. Now she's not doing her homework, failing her tests," he groused one night.

"She's suddenly uncommunicative, refuses to talk to her mother about anything" was the follow-up complaint.

Another night Daddy divulged, "She broke her curfew. She's starting to defy Melissa, to stay out late."

Starting? Hello—if Daddy only knew.

"She's doing everything in her power to drive her mother nuts," Daddy concluded, shaking his head and throwing up his hands in disgust.

I offered, "It's classic. Tara's just trying to get Melissa's attention. She wants her to . . . maybe not go out so much?"

He sighed. "We've thought of that, Cher. We're trying to be sensitive to her feelings, but we can't allow her to manipulate us."

Two pronouns—"we" and "us"—in such close proximity was unnerving.

Daddy continued, "Tara's just going to have to get used to the fact that her mother's in a relationship now. A good one."

On Thursday I dressed for my picking-up-De's-excess-boyage date, relieved to be excused from Tara tales for the night.

77

Irony alert: Later I would think that might, after all, have been preferable.

It ended up being the double date from boredom hell. Generously, De allowed me to choose the dude I wanted. Okay, so normally, I have a rule about not going out with boys who are prettier than I am. But who *wouldn't* jump at a chance with Philippe, studmuffin shopping bag supermodel?

Note: even off the shopping bag, Philippe did not disappoint. He was jaw-droppingly Baldwin.

Grievously, he was also jaw-droppingly self-absorbed and accessorized with a room-temperature IQ. Over rabbit food at Crustacean, a trendy must-be-seenerie, he was all "Let's talk about me." His attitude was matched only by Diego's swimming-through-Jell-O, duh-head superficiality.

Okay, so I totally pride myself on not believing in stereotypes. But both of them were fully model. After thirty excruciating minutes, I was over Philippe's looks.

How I longed for a kabob of wit. The gift of goofy. An explosion of citrus. Murray.

Grievously, the chasm between Murray and De was widening. Not unlike the San Andreas fault. I'd counseled De, "Wait it out, he'll come crawling back," but so far? Murray wasn't even thinking knee bend, let alone considering the crawl. Direct intervention was called for. It was way ASAP-y.

The next day I passed a note to Murray to meet me in the hallway by the Guidance Office between first and second period. We'd have some privacy there, since that office is only sporadically used. Most Bronson Alcott students get guidance from high-priced shrinks and private college counselors.

When Murray showed up—looking dapper, yet drab—I had an entire speech ready. On how he's making this huge mistake. How he made such the wrong turn on Relationship Drive. How he could hang a U-ie and go back to De.

Murray listened calmly. When I was done, he stroked his chin and let out a long sigh. Bad sign. So I tossed in, "De's the best thing that ever happened to you, Murray. You used to know that."

Finally, he spoke. "Key phrase, Cher: Used to. We *used to* be freshmen. We *used to* think Joanie and Chachi would live happily ever after. I *used to* be into Pac-Man. But I grew up. We all did."

I bristled, because I knew Murray was regurgitating Richard-rhetoric. "So you're saying that all of a sudden, without any outside influence, you suddenly outgrew De, fully the hottest Betty in Bronson Alcott, a stellar physician-to-be? How could you even compare her to a gobbling yellow orb in a computer game?"

Murray tapped his foot impatiently. I couldn't help noticing boring brown Bally loafers were where colorful Hush Puppies used to live. "Look, Cher, De's a great woman. I have nothing but respect for her. But she's my past. If I didn't break it off now, we would end up being together forever."

"Hello, is that so wrong?"

"I would have missed out on the whole dating

scene, an integral part of my growing-up experience."

I countered, "But isn't the whole point of dating to find the right person? Isn't that why we go through this awkward, often random ritual? And if you find the right person early, it's like instant promotion. You get to skip all the Mr. and Ms. Wrongs."

Murray shifted uncomfortably. The shoes were pinching his toes. And, adjunct: his brain. "I gotta look to the future, Cher. Richard had it right. Breaking up with De now was a good thing. The right thing."

As if. To other ears, Murray spouted convincing, but a total t.b. knows hesitation when she hears it. I would have called him on it—but that's when we both heard it. A teen-slasher-flick-worthy scream! It came from down the hallway.

Okay, so I didn't need to rush to the site to know *who* it was: but even I wouldn't have guessed *why* Mt. Saint Amber had erupted in a volcanic hissy fit.

Murray and I dashed down the corridor only to see Coach Diemer and Principal Lehrer grasping Amber's elbows in an attempt to restrain her. Amber was fighting all the way. When she saw me, she turned the volume up on her shrieking. "Cher, you have to stop them! They're calling my parents! This cannot happen!"

I was alarmed. Our school never calls anyone's parents! That is so Valley.

Murray, confused as I was, asked, "What'd she do?"

Principal Lehrer informed us, "It's not what she did. It's what she wore."

The school was taking action—after all these years—on Amber's inane costumes?

Coach Diemer, who finally had a vise-grip on Amber's arm, barked, "Marins! Show Horowitz and Duvall what you wore to school."

Slowly, Amber opened her palm to display the offensive accessories. Displaying officious optic verve, she'd worn hand-painted contact lenses to school. She'd finagled the lenses out of her neighbor, a horror movie special effects expert. In her incognito delirium, Amber had chosen yellow vampire contact lenses. As Coach explained, they caused seizures in anyone who looked at her—luckily, her unpopularity kept that number to a minimum. Still, the school had branded Amber a health hazard.

I had to step in. "I'll take responsibility for her, Principal Lehrer."

Coach Diemer barked, "Good intentions, Horowitz. But impractical. You're not her guardian. We're trying to contact her parents."

I shrugged. "It's your call, but you could be stuck with her all day. Dr. Marins is probably in deep session with some delusional movie mogul who claims to be king of the world. And Mrs. Dr. Marins is running the Ladies Who Kvetch Bowling League."

I paused. That I even knew Amber's parents' schedule proved I'd known the entire family too long. "I'll take her home and make her change her lenses."

Murray vouched for my responsibility before dashing off to his class.

Amber was wriggling out of Coach's grip. Out of exasperation mainly, our PE teacher and Principal Lehrer agreed to let me handle her.

In the car, Amber wailed, "Not home! Anyplace but home!"

"Don't say it, Amber—you're not coming to my house."

Okay, so her vampire contact lens tears got to me. Knowing I'd fully regret my actions, I made a right, toward my house.

On the ride home, out of desperation, I vented my frustration about the De-Murray split. "Neither one is following his or her own heart. Murray is taking advice from his puffed-up pretentious cousin, and De's allowing her pride to get in the way of her real feelings. It's all so obvious. Why can't they see it?"

Amber leaned back in the seat and closed her eyes. "If you allow people to follow their hearts, bad things happen. My real parents are trying to find me. And your real father is following his heart—it's about to play havoc with your life."

"Only you could leap from the impossible to the inane. Speaking of which, you've carried this charade way past its amusing stage. Cease the despair, Amber. No one's trying to find you."

I was surprised to see Daddy's car in the driveway. He used to work from home a lot, but not since Melissa. He must have heard us come in, because he was waiting in the foyer. I explained about our unscheduled early departure from school.

He shrugged. "Well, I was going to wait until this afternoon, but as long as you're here . . . uh, Cher, can I speak to you in private?"

Amber waved us off. "I'm going up to collapse. It has been a traumatic morning." As she lumbered upstairs, I followed Daddy into his study. That's when I noticed how fidgety he was. He paced his study, patting the chair.

"Sit down, sweetheart."

My radar went up. "What is it, Daddy? Is it something bad?"

"No, no, honey, this is good news."

I sank into the chair and immediately brightened. "My room! You've decided to let me expand into the Cher wing!"

"Better than that. Melissa and I have decided to get married."

Chapter 8

Sputtering, stuttering, and stammering are not my normal afflictions, but Daddy's "Iceberg! Iceberg ahead!" shocker resulted in instant articulation impairment. The best I could manage was "Why?"

It wasn't the reaction Daddy had hoped for. He took a deep breath and went back to pacing. In measured tones he said, "You want to know why. Well, honey, people at my age get married for a variety of reasons. Sometimes, it's just for companionship. For the lucky ones, it's love. For the luckiest ones, it's love for the second time around."

The category Daddy thought he and Melissa fell into was all over his face.

Flabbergasted was all over mine. And okay, I know I should have been more gracious, but I couldn't stop the whine. "But, Daddy, how can you be sure? You only just started dating."

Abruptly, he stopped pacing and sat down on the couch next to me. He took my hand and looked into my eyes. "Maybe it's because we are older, wiser, more mature. We recognize real love when we feel it. And we also know that life is short. When you're given this gift—at this stage—you act on it."

We both thought of famous three-word poems at the same time. Mine was "Fools rush in."

His was "Now or never."

To which he added, "Those words take on special meaning as you age."

Then he hugged me. "This just feels right, Cher. We're following our hearts. Say you'll give us your blessing."

I mumbled something about a blessing—but it might have been the one over the candles at Hanukkah. I was fully in a daze when I tottered out of Daddy's study. My instinct was to go to my room and call De, but I paused at the bottom of the steps. Mom's portrait.

I looked deeply into her eyes, captured for all eternity in the glitter blue eye shadow of the disco era. Even then Mom probably knew that such a classic makeup style would come back. She had to know what was up with Daddy. I had to know what she thought. I said, "Daddy wouldn't take this plunge without consulting you. Bizarre turn of events alert. Are you okay with this?"

I'm an expert at interpreting Mom's opinions. At least I thought I was. But every way I looked at

Mom—from the right, the left, down and up, up and down—her eyes remained fixed on me. And they told me she was okay with it.

Before going back to school, I assured Mom that no matter what happens, the dining room table was staying. And her portrait was so not moving from its exalted bottom of the staircase place. Even if I had to stand guard over it.

Grievously, Amber slept over that night. Maybe the proximity of Her Weirdness caused my bizarro dream. Or maybe it was the real life events of the past few weeks.

I dreamed I was in an off-white Narciso Rodriguez organza gown. My silky hair was in a furious up-do. I was in a huge ballroom, doing what I do best: being in charge. I was giving directions to the wait staff, greeting guests, accepting compliments on the decor, the theme, the profound pageantry of the event. Totally everyone was there. All Daddy's big name clients, including Jerry Springer and Oprah. It was beyond Oscar, beyond MTV Rock N' Jock, or any disease-oriented charity function. This was the social event of the season.

And then the band started playing. The song was "Lawyers in Love."

And then I saw Daddy. He was in the stellar Prada tux I'd chosen for him. The scene changed, and he took my hand and started leading me down this aisle. At the end, under the chuppah, was . . . not Leonardo for me, but . . . Melissa for him. And there was Tara—dressed in my poufy pink curtains!—by her side. As I drew closer, Tara whispered snarkily, "Do you like what I did with your curtains? I've painted your room. Black. Sister."

I woke up in a cold sweat. My heart was pounding profusely. I took several deep calming breaths, dabbed the back of my neck with aromatherapy lotion, and repeated the mantra "It's only a dream. It's only a dream."

After I washed up, I tried to rouse Amber, but she waved me off. "It's Saturday, leave me alone. And FYI, Cher: whatever nightmare you were raving about before? It wasn't only a dream."

I stifled the urge to suffocate her, but only because of the stain her green masque would leave on my pillowcase.

When I came down for breakfast, Daddy was whistling jauntily. He gave me a peck on my head. "I have some news I think you're going to like, Cher," he said merrily.

"You've changed your mind about marrying Melissa?" Okay, so I didn't say that. But I thought it. Loudly.

Not loudly enough. Daddy munched his toast and mused, "You know that Cher Wing you've been bugging me about? I've decided it's a good idea, after all. With our family expanding, we'll need to use more rooms in the house. You can start thinking about decorating, and Tara can move into your room."

I tensed. "They're moving in? Tara's getting my room? When was all this decided?" When did my nightmare become reality?

Daddy tilted his head and gave me a funny look. "That's all right, isn't it? I mean, you don't want to move, do you? And Melissa's thrilled. It means Tara will go to Bronson Alcott and get a fresh start."

I blurted, "As if! And my room will get a fresh coat of paint!"

Daddy was perplexed. "Cher, you've been nagging me for a new suite of rooms. I thought you'd be thrilled."

I swallowed. "I . . . I'm just . . . maybe I'll keep my room. She can have the west wing. All to herself."

And then maybe I'll never have to see her.

Daddy sighed and shook his head. "I don't get it, Cher. I thought you'd be thrilled. What's going on? Is there something you're not telling me?"

Avoiding eye contact, I assured him I was not withholding.

But Daddy wasn't fully buying it. He cupped my chin, forcing me to look at him. "You're okay with what I told you yesterday, right? About Melissa and me getting married? Because if you're not, Cher, we should talk about it."

A fork in the road. I could have told Daddy my real feelings, but hello, what were they, even? Ambivalence ruled.

So I slapped a smile on my face and went with the road more trampled. "Doy, Daddy, why would I not be okay with it? You and Melissa are rampantly right for each other. Anyone could see that. I guess I just wasn't expecting a wedding so soon. That is."

My voice wavered, but Daddy didn't catch it. He beamed. "How did I get so lucky to have you as a daughter? You are so level-headed. So mature. And you have such a good heart, Cher. You get that all from your mother."

Suddenly, I sensed that Daddy was about to segue into Tara. I abruptly got up from the table, explaining, "De and I are having a major girl-bonding sleepover tonight, and, uh, I've got to get supplies."

Daddy arched his eyebrows. "Just the two of you?"

I paused, remembering the drama queen snoring upstairs. "I wish. But somehow Amber will find a way to join us."

"In that case, why not invite Tara?"

A million reasons came to mind—not the least of which was "I can't stand her." But I didn't say anything. Daddy was waiting for a response.

Finally, I sputtered, "I—I don't think that would . . . make sense. I mean, at some point, but right now the timing is *so* not great. De's in a state of full denial over Murray dumping her. And Amber's fully mental."

A sly smile spread over Daddy's face. "Then Tara will fit right in."

He paused. "Just kidding. But really, Cher, this could be just what Tara needs. You and your friends will be a good influence on her. And besides, you girls might as well start—what do you call it? Bonding? You will be living under the same roof soon. You'll be sisters."

"Step—" I started, but Daddy overruled me. "Step one: have her over. Make her feel like one of the gang."

I protested, "Bad plan, Daddy. I mean, we'll fully

89

do it. We'll . . . bond. Tara and I. Just not tonight. Besides, hello, late notice! I'm sure she has plans."

"I'm sure she doesn't. She's grounded."

I shrugged. "Even more reason. Who am I to interfere with her grounding? She'll sleep over another time."

Not even. Once Daddy latches onto an idea, he goes profoundly pit bull. "Invite her, Cher. Do it for me, for the future of our family. I want this to work, and I know you do too. Besides, it's just one little sleep-over. It's not the apocalypse."

Later, as I was multi-tasking, poring over munchie and video choices for the night, I called De and crabbed about Tara. "Who invited her into my life?"

De, who hadn't been hugely empathetic lately, answered my rhetorical question. "Apparently, your father did. Without consulting you. Much the same as Murray forced me into life changes. But you've got to move on, Cher. Let it sink in, accept it, and move forward. I did."

"But, De, bad comparison. This is not some temporary insanity thing that Murray caught from his cousin. This signals a seismic shift in my lifestyle."

De clicked off with, "Words of advice, girlfriend: nothing lasts forever."

By the time I called Tara with the forced-on-me invite, Daddy had already forewarned Melissa. Who in turn ensured that Tara would accept. During our fully brief conversation, I didn't broach the subject of our parents' stealth wedding decision. But, hello, you didn't have to be that famous cartoon shrink, Dr. Katz, Professional Therapist, to know Tara wasn't happy about it.

How happy she *wasn't* was crystal clear when she showed up later for the sleep-over. Tara had reacted to the wedding news with a fashion statement.

She'd shaved her head.

Chapter 9

My mortified reaction when I flung open our front door was: Even Gwen wouldn't go that far! I couldn't say *that*, but I had to say something. I went with a jumbled mumble about "the ultimate solution to bad hair days."

Tara's victorious grin as she brushed by me with her duffel bag slung over her shoulder answered my silent question about what her mother had had to say. Melissa was probably sobbing on Daddy's shoulder right now.

The two of them had left early to go to a cocktail party. Before leaving, Daddy had gone wholly uncharacteristic. I mean, in all our seventeen years together, Daddy's never said stuff like "Don't do this." Or "You can't." Or even that famous parental chant "Because I said so." Our relationship is way more evolved than that. But now that Tara's in the picture, it's like one giant step backward for all of Horowitz-kind.

"Tara's under house arrest," Daddy informed me sheepishly. "Melissa asked that you please all stay put for the night. No going out."

Okay, a field trip wasn't on the agenda, but being told we couldn't was furiously annoying. And protest-worthy. "When did I become Tara's keeper? This is woefully unfair."

Wearily, Daddy said, "Please don't argue with me, Cher." Then he totally turned that profound advertising slogan against me: "Just do it."

Whatever. One look at Tara's stubbly scalp and like, who'd want to be seen with her? Even Sinead O'Connor in her ripping-the-pontiff's-picture moment and Demi as GI Jane made a more convincing fashion statement.

De, who thankfully arrived soon after, barely blinked at Tara's chrome dome. She toted her Vuitton luggage set upstairs to my room and repaired to my dressing area to change into her evening wear ensemble: a Victoria's Secret teddy. Okay, so to some Bettys that would have been a righteous selection, but De never dresses that way. DKNY sweats are her normal slumber-party attire. My take? The Murray dumping had informed her every move.

Then, she planted herself on the plush pink carpet and began setting up for the night. De had brought a full smorgasbord of nail polish hues for our manicures and pedicures. She'd also done a full swipe of the Bobbi Brown counter at Neiman's, leaving no eye or lip shade unexplored. My generous main had brought possibilities for all four of us, even Tara-come-lately.

Amber, who hadn't left my room all day, stayed in character—viciously unappreciative. She sat next to De and disdainfully picked up each bottle of nail polish, making faces. "This is the best you could do? Fetish shades? What, I ask, am I even doing here?"

My question exactly. For Tara.

Without asking, Tara had claimed my beanbag hassock and was using it like a toy horse, bouncing around the room on it. Like she lived here already.

Fuming at her insolence, I went, "Tara? Do you mind? You're denting my carpet." That was so lame, even De and Amber reacted like I'd lost it.

But Tara merely shifted onto my bed and began extracting stuff from her duffel. I panicked. If I so much as saw one flash of an illegal substance, I was beeping Daddy. No way was she putting us at risk again.

But nothing illegal emerged from Tara's tote. Just heinous. As in, her clothes. For slumber-party chic, Ms. Baldie had decided to go with camouflage drawstrings and cut-off belly-ring-revealing crop-top—the same outfit she'd been in the night we met. As if I needed a visual reminder.

Whatever. Somehow, I would not let her—or Amber—get to me. I would massively accomplish the goal of this night. De and I would girlfriend bond, and then, when we had some privacy, I'd gently steer her out of Denial-ville. I'd get her to see that she really wants Murray back. And then we'd figure out how.

Now that I'd refocused, I donned my ensemble for the night: brushed cotton cloud and sheep PJs—only the cutting-edge nightwear of the moment, popularized by Ally McBeal.

Surprisingly, no one noticed and/or gave me props. Except Tara. She remarked, "When does the Ooga-chocka baby appear?"

In spite of myself, I grinned. And thought: if I *could* conjure up computer-generated Baby Cha Cha, I'd have him aim an arrow straight at you and knock you off my bed.

Just then our front door chimes rang. I assumed it signaled delivery of the 'za from Spago, Beverly Hills. But not even. Two beefy dudes were at the door, hauling not recyclable cardboard pizza boxes but a trunk. Hello—Amber thinks she's moving in? As if!

I was about to tell them, "Wrong address," when Amber materialized behind me. Pointing up the staircase, she commanded, "Take it up there, fellas. Second door on the left. And try not to drop it, okay?"

As they lugged the trunk up the stairs, she turned to me. "Got any spare change for a tip? Something tells me Amex gold is not the currency on their home planet."

Fully fuming, I tipped the delivery men in cash and ushered them out. Then I stomped back upstairs.

De, who'd stuck cotton balls between her toes in pedicure prep, regarded Amber's trunk and noted, "Tactical error, undercover Amber. Won't your real parents be able to track you here by following the trunk trail?"

I couldn't believe De was, like, encouraging her delusion. Amber threw her a disgusted look. "You think I had this delivered here first? This trunk, packed with my necessities—amenities are seriously lacking around here—has been delivered to three different destinations tonight. No one will track it."

"But your parents—Dr. and Mrs. Marins, that is—know you're here?" I dreaded the answer.

Amber carefully unlocked her trunk and started sifting through her stuff. "As if! They think I'm with cousin Ashley—who, unbeknownst to them, happens to be out of the country. They'll never check."

Then she whipped out her plumage-obsessed peignoir and cuddled it. "I've missed you."

I looked around my bedroom. De had started to do an undercoat on her toes. She had her game face on, as if Murray had never iced the relationship.

Amber was hugging her trunk.

Tara, the bald brat, had claimed the remote and was channel surfing.

A telememory came to me. It was that song from *Sesame Street*. The one where they give you four pictures and you have to pick the one that doesn't match. As a toddler, I totally ruled that game.

I still do. What was now wrong with the picture in my room was: only everything.

And then all of a sudden, that memory jolted me into the reality zone. I, Cher Horowitz, embrace challenges. I celebrate challenges. I define solutions.

So De was distraught *and* in denial? Nothing I couldn't fix.

So Amber was, like, here? Totally time-lock. She'll be gone soon.

So Tara was . . . okay, not going there. Just yet.

Brightly, I chirped, "Who's hungry? I've stocked up on all the major munchie food groups—olestra chips, air-popped popcorn, sushi, California rolls, thirst-quenching drinks . . ."

No one even looked up. Whatever. If the girl-friends won't go to the munchies, I'll bring the munchies to them.

The finger-food fest, complemented with the swift arrival of the pizza, plus a diva-driven musical sound track—everyone from Aretha to Mariah to Shania—proved such the stress antidote. It soothed our souls and moved us into girlfriend-bonding sync.

Amber busied herself unpacking, then got on her cell phone and started ordering stuff from catalogs. No matter how many times I scolded, "This is not your new address, Ambu-lunatic," I had to keep grabbing the phone to stop her from having anything delivered here.

De and I did each other's nails. As I worked on her, I tried to casually steer the conversation toward the bore-a-holic double date we'd gone on. Somehow I'd get her to admit the error of generic hottie hunts.

Tara had the TV on the entire time. I couldn't be sure, but I think she was flipping between Nick at Nite and the Food Network.

After De and I finished our manicures, I decided

it was time for a movie. I held up our video selections and described. "The Julia Roberts curly-tressed classics collection: *Pretty Woman* and *My Best Friend's Wedding.* Or we could do studmuffin eye-candy: Matt and Ben in *Good Will Hunting* or Antonio as *Zorro.* Or . . . all Leo, all the time—*Titanic* and *Romeo + Juliet.*"

Amber, who relates to devious Julia in *My Best Friend's Wedding,* voted for that, but De and I longed for our Leo. I looked to Tara as a potential tiebreaker.

"I have a better idea," she announced, doing a belly flop on my bed. She reached over for her duffel, which was now on the floor.

"Don't even think of it," I warned, panicked that she'd pull out a box of smokes.

But instead of grabbing a cigarette, she went for a fistful of popcorn from the bowl next to her bag and shoved it into her mouth. "Forget videos. Let's do something interactive. Let's play Truth or Dare."

I rolled my eyes. "Hello, that is so *Dawson's Creek.*"

Tara taunted me, "What's the matter, Cher, you afraid?"

"Afraid? Of what?" I didn't bother adding that my fully icky nightmare was already heinously unfolding before my eyes. What else was there to be afraid of?

Amber spoke up. Malevolently. "I like it. Good idea, Tara. An improvement over the shaved head statement. Have you considered a wig?"

At Tara's glare, Amber amended, "Just a suggestion. Anyway, I'll go first."

My objections were overruled.

Amber turned to De. Correction: turned *on* De. "Truth or dare, Dionne."

De blew on her still-drying nails and, unafraid, answered, "Truth."

Amber's expression was pure evil. "You want Murray back."

Tiny beads of sweat spontaneously erupted on De's forehead. I knew the rash was starting on her back, too.

De tried to appear nonchalant. She blew more forcefully on her nails. Finally, she stated, "No, I don't want Murray back."

Amber bolted over and squatted next to De. They were eye-to-contacts. "Excuse me, I believe you said truth."

De turned away, bristling. "Murray did me a favor. One I was about to bestow on him. He beat me to the punch is all. I do not want him back." Then she blew like this hurricane force gale wind on her nails.

Amber grabbed De's chin and stared her down. "May I remind you—under the rules of this game, you are under oath. Truth."

And that's when it happened. De blinked. A tear escaped. And then another. In the tiniest whisper, she confessed, "Okay, maybe. I do."

T.b. 911! I bolted over to her. Displaying Xena strength, I pulled De up and hustled her into my dressing room. I would not allow my main to suffer Ambu-miliation in front of Tara.

I slammed the door behind us and comforted her. "De, it's okay. I know."

She sobbed, "I tried not to care. I tried to see the

99

bright side, to move on. I mean, hello, this is me! No boy has ever left me."

"And Murray didn't either—not of his own volition. It's just his insecurity. You said it yourself. For some reason, he's been brainwashed by Richard. But he'll come back, De."

Her eyes welled with tears. She croaked bitterly. "What if he doesn't?"

"Tscha! You'll get him back, De. We will *so* see to it."

De shot me a crooked little smile. Doubtful, but encouraged.

I motioned to the door. "But, hello, priorities. We have something more immediate on our agenda: Getting back at Amber. Let's make *her* do a truth or dare. And we so know where her weak spots are."

De grinned, and I gave her an extra-ply tissue. She wiped her eyes so hard that all the new makeup came off. She shrugged. "This color was so not happening."

"All repaired?" Amber cracked as we returned to the bedroom. "Looks like I touched a little nerve there, didn't I?" She did a faux wrist slap. "Bad Amber."

De eyeballed her. "Your turn. Truth or dare, Amber. How many nose jobs, oh, queen of rhinoplastic reconstruction?"

Amber turned her current nose up. "Anyone with an ounce of class would never divulge that."

I cracked, "Which lets you out. So, that week you were ostensibly at tennis camp . . . surgeon's office, right?"

Amber folded her arms, obstinately refusing to answer. We continued to goad her. Finally, she sighed, "What*ever*. Dare."

De licked her lips. "Good, now we're getting somewhere. I dare you to confront your parents. Tragically, though we all *wish* otherwise, you are so *not* missing. They'll confirm it, and we'll be spared your histrionics."

I high-fived De as she shoved the phone at Amber.

Amber huffed, "No way! They'll tell the truth. And where will I be then?"

Tara chimed in, "Sorry, Amber, you said dare. You have to. Call them."

Amber started to stalk away. "I'll do it tomorrow."

But Tara jumped off the bed and collared her. "Look, Red, I don't know you very well. Nor do I particularly want to. But in the spirit of the game, do this. And if you won't confront your own parents— hire my mother. Like I told you, the missing child business is what she does. It's not like you can't afford her fee."

Amber quivered. "But what if she finds out that the face on the milk carton *was* me? And those . . . *people* . . . want me back?"

Tara ran her hand over her shiny pate. "How dense are you? Why do you assume you'll be forced back? You're seventeen, above the age of consent. They'll ask you where you want to live."

Amber considered. "Okay. It's a deal. Tomorrow. I'll hire your mother."

Then Tara suddenly spun around to me. "I like this game. It's time for you, Cher. Truth or dare."

I met her stare. "Hit me with your best shot, Tara."

Oops. What was I thinking?

Because Tara went for it. Brutally. "Truth or dare: You don't want your father to marry my mother."

A hush fell over the room. De, Amber, and Tara eyeballed me. But, excuse me, how could I answer honestly? I didn't even know how I felt about it. And if I did? Share with her? As if. She wasn't De, my main t.b. Or Murray or Sean. She wasn't even Amber. All she was was some bald faux Gwen wannabe who might get my room.

But I couldn't say all that. I gulped. "Dare."

The grin that spread across Tara's face was massively mischievous. She rubbed her hands together and declared, "We're breaking out of here."

I folded my arms across my chest. "Objection. We're not going anywhere."

Tara stared at me levelly. "Overruled. Cher, you *said* dare. And this is my dare. I dare you to come with me. You have to do it. And besides, you were about to watch that excruciating excuse for a movie, *Titanic,* because of Leo. You want Leo? I'm taking you where you can get Leo—in the flesh."

Instantly, De lit up. "Really?"

I knew what she was thinking: if Murray ever found out she met Leo, he'd be furiously jealous. Insanely jealous. Jealous enough to come crawling back.

Nonchalantly, Tara added, "Club Metro is Leo's hangout. And I don't know about you, but I miss the place—I haven't been there, in, oh, days! I dare you to come with me. All of you."

Tragically? I needed Amber as an ally.

Heinously, she refused.

Her reasoning? "Club Metro? That downmarket dive overpopulated with whiny wannabes and pathetic hangers-on? No one will *ever* think to look for me there!"

Stubbornly, I continued to resist. Besides all the obvious reasons for not wanting to make a repeat appearance there, Daddy had decreed, "No going out." Because Tara was under house arrest. Exactly why the bald brat was pushing for it.

All three of them were looking at me. Profound peer pressure alert!

Amber taunted, "Party pooper."

Tara teased, "Goody Two-shoes."

De shot me a besieging look. "Come on, Cher, it'll be major. A Leo sighting would be pretty incredible, no? Something to tell your grandchildren."

I was mega-wiggin'. At, like, everyone. If Richard hadn't influenced Murray, he wouldn't have broken up with De, and she wouldn't need to side with Tara, the teen ogre.

If Amber hadn't descended into the depths of madness, she'd be anywhere but here.

And if Daddy hadn't deputized me the boss of Tara, I wouldn't be in this profoundly precarious position.

Daddy had put me here. He deserved it if we did go out. Whatever the consequences.

Chapter 10

I needed an ensemble to match my mood. Daring, yet designer. I chose a screaming red Galliano tube top shift and red suede stacked Manolos. I redid my hair to form a zigzag part. My fashion statement: reckless yet ragin'.

Amber extracted a sleeveless metallic dress from her trunk, snarkily announcing, "Had you been to the Milan show, you would know that retro with techno metallics are the trend."

"You look like the Tin Man, Amber," I retorted. "Fashion-challenged and heartless. The complete package."

De rolled her eyes at Amber and sashayed over to my closet. After a quick computer consult, she borrowed my Bisou-Bisou floral miniskirt and paired it with my faux leopard collared cardigan. By adding ankle-grazing Coach boots, she owned the look. Even in deepest dumpee grief, De could do stellar, fully unparalleled.

And then there was Tara, who continued to look follicularly challenged.

All my instincts screamed "head wrap!" "Want to adopt an accessory? I have a full selection of hats, baseball caps, scarves, extensions . . ."

Tara glanced at me coolly. "I don't need anything from you, Cher."

Petulantly, I refused to drive, so we all piled into De's Infiniti convertible. It was fully uncanny, I thought, what a potential Leo sighting could do. My main had gone from glum to glam to gleeful in, like, a nanosecond. As she turned onto Sunset in the direction of Club Metro, loudly and off-key, she began warbling that Paula Cole TV theme song classic, "I Don't Want to Wait." Tara and Amber took turns chiming in on the "doo-doo-doo-doo-doos."

"We probably won't even get in," I yelled over their singing, hoping that without Richard's connections, we'd be turned away by the club's bouncers. But grievously, Tara had her own connections. She waved at the brawny bouncer, who welcomed her with a wink. "Hey, Tara!" he said. "Love the new 'do, darlin'! Right this way, ladies." Then he did that Moses-at-Passover thing, parting the red velvet ropes.

Club Metro was grievously déjà view: exactly as I remembered it. Chokingly smoky, drearily dark, crushingly crowded, obscenely loud as a Marilyn

Manson/Smash Mouth mix rocked the room. And post mortem: it was time to play Name That Smell. Club Metro was way olfactory-challenged.

Tragically, we scored a table right away, in the middle of the floor. In a way fire hazard manner, we were totally on top of our neighbors. To Tara that was a plus. She seemed to know them, although thankfully I didn't see her biker-babe cohorts from our debut encounter.

I nudged De to commiserate about the discomfort factor, but she was glowing, scanning the room for celebrities. Even Amber was into it, bellowing satisfaction. "No one would ever think to look for me here. This is foul! Fierce! But brilliant."

Eventually, the waiter ambled over. Before Tara could get us into any more trouble, I made a preemptive strike and ordered four iced teas. Tara snickered at me, shook her hairless head, and went back to her conversation with a scary-looking group at the next table.

I elbowed De. "Tell me again why we're here?"

De responded by bouncing up and down in her seat and pointing to a table in the darkest corner of the club, nearly obscured by the bar. "This is why we're here," she burbled in a timbre several decibels above her normal. "Got a camera?"

"De, what the . . ." I started to ask, but she shrieked, "It's *him*—at that table, the one surrounded by bodyguards! Cher, I have to get my picture taken with him!"

"No way, De." I started to get up for a better view of the bodyguard-obsessed star, but all I could make out was a he-waif in a baseball cap. A flick of blond hair escaped from under the brim.

Could it really be? I leaned around De for another angle, but just then three things happened at once.

A waiter bearing our drinks on a tray approached.

A loud crashing sound thundered over the Smash Mouth sound track.

A furious herd of camera-wielding paparazzi stampeded through the door.

And okay, so Chaos? It was no longer just a DKNY fragrance. The dictionary definition—confusion, turmoil, pandemonium—reigned.

A wave of panic swept over me. Hyperventilating, I screamed, "Our cue, girlfriends: on three, we bail!" I started to count, and grabbed De's arm to pull her up—but she resisted, shouting, "No, wait, I want to see if it's Leo!"

Amber and Tara stayed glued to their seats, fully invested in the erupting fracas. While Amber seemed stunned, Tara's eyes sparkled. She was into it.

I was caught in a quagmire. Should I leave and save myself? Or should I be such the captain of my erstwhile sleep-over and go down with my guests? I was faced with a mega Shoppie's Choice.

Grievously, I dawdled too long in the quagmire. For just then a troika of thug-esque bodyguards came charging from the back of the room, straight at the paparazzi, who, in turn, scattered like a pearl necklace dropped on marble tiles.

Tragically, one corpulent cameraman got knocked backward into our table, tipping it all the way over. Arms flailing, he also managed to wipe out the waiter carrying our drinks. Upshot: all four iced teas splattered on my crimson Galliano.

"How rude!" I screamed, grabbing for a bunch of napkins. De sprung into action, steadying the table first, then pushing the offending photographer out of the way before he could do more damage.

Tara and Amber rose, too, but not to help. They stubbornly insisted on getting a glimpse of the star at the center of the storm. Brazenly, they pushed their way right into the bodyguard-paparazzi confrontation. De and I rushed after them, attempting to stop them, but I suddenly felt someone shove me and step on my toe. I went ballistic. "That was a suede Manolo!"

And then the whole room went white. While it was an improvement over the drabness, I went temporarily blind. Camera flashes popped in my eyes, and intense screaming filled my ears.

It took a full second before I realized it was Amber, whose shrieking could summon lost pets all over the Southland. She was profoundly postal: "No pictures, you animal! Give me that film!"

Blinking, I regained my eyesight just in time to see her lunge at a random paparazzo, trying to grab his camera.

Hello, backfire alert. Amber's hissy fit only attracted the other shutterbugs, who—thinking she must be "someone"—aimed their high-powered lenses at her and began shooting away.

Addendum: Amber's antics separated the t.b.'s from the not-t.b.'s.

Tara, such the not, took in the whole scene, preening and posing. She was grooving on every minute of it, no doubt relishing the major aggro she could further cause her mother.

De, who *is* a t.b., and—okay—spurred on by *any* confrontation, took Amber's side. She whirled toward the foul photographer, swinging at anyone in her path and demanding, "You heard her! Hand over the film!"

I was about to go to Amber's aid, too, but suddenly, someone yelled, "Forget her! We lost him!"

In a flash, the whole paparazzi pack flew out of the club. The upshot? Aside from my fully trashed ensemble, stacked heels included, Amber had inadvertently created a diversion, during which the real Leo—or whoever the babe in the baseball cap was—made his escape.

We made ours immediately after. Just before the police arrived.

Serendipitously, Daddy and Melissa weren't back when we got home. They never saw our sorry, soiled state. By the time they did amble in, we were showered, pajama clad, and safely tucked in.

But not asleep. I heard Daddy whisper to Melissa, "See, they're all there. I told you Cher was responsible. I bet they had a great time and they're all friends now."

Tara's words rumbled at me: "What my mother doesn't know won't hurt her." It pained me to agree with her, but a higher truth prevailed: the pain would be more intense if her mother and/or my daddy ever did find out what really happened tonight. Whatever. Closing credits had rolled. No one got hurt or detained. So how could they find out?

Naive assumption alert. It was all, where there's paparazzi, there's the *National Tabloid*. And when people you know are *in* the rag-mags, it beats two-headed aliens or even precious pictures of identically clad septuplets. Our entire school was National Tabloid–armed the following Monday morning.

I'd barely gotten out of my car when De and Amber materialized. De shoved a copy of the offensive newspaper at me. "Look what Sean gave me. It's all over the school."

The photos were fully heinous. Flashbulbs in dark clubs are so not the lighting a Betty ever wants to be captured in. And yet, there we were: me, De, Amber, and braying, bald Tara, such the Bambi-Bettys caught in the headlights. And, adjunct: the headlines: "Chaos at Club Metro! Leo Eludes Photographers, While High School Girl Causes Melee."

My cellular rang all day. Grumpily, I answered, "Humiliation Central." We were the finger-pointing snicker talk of Bronson Alcott. It would have been heinously humbling, massively mortifying, seriously shameful even. But like that famous poem about the silver trimming in the clouds? I know what I saw.

Via a series of sidelong glances, Murray regarded

De differently. With new respect. With awe. With a soupçon of yearning.

He wanted her back. Not that he knew it yet. But he would.

As the day wore on, I chilled. I mean, whatever. For one thing, Daddy doesn't go to our school, and his daily newspapers are the *LA Times* and the *Wall Street Journal*. Papers that could be counted on not to cover our Club Metro bad.

Ergo, he'll never know. And hello, soon it would be replaced by some new scandal. Surely some new Robert Downey Jr. or Christian Slater or other random bimbo or himbo eruption would claim the *Hard Copy* headlines. I mean, if nothing else, *somewhere* Bobby Brown is punching out a photographer. Tomorrow it will all be forgotten. Like Sandra Bullock's career.

Grievously? It was still today when I got home. Where Daddy was waiting. Clutching the *National Tabloid*. My tummy went into full-tilt turbulence.

Daddy was beet-faced; his mood, fuming. Yet, he didn't explode right away. Silence is so not golden. It's more like . . . bronze alloy.

Finally, just as I tried to get past him to rush upstairs, he let it out, booming, "We all know Tara's got issues. But *you*, Cher! I thought you were above this. I asked you to do one thing for me. I distinctly remember telling you to stay in Saturday night, did I not? How could you let this happen?"

I would have answered, but I know a rhetorical question when I hear one.

Daddy was into tumultuous thundering. "You're

grounded, Cher! To your room—now! Do not come out until it's time for school tomorrow."

By grounding me, Daddy had given me the gift of pondering-time. I used it well. I meditated. I visualized. I waxed.

Daddy was right. Normally, I was above this. Normally, I wouldn't allow myself to be influenced by anyone as style-challenged, morose, and bald as Tara. I would have tried to steer her toward a healthier way to express herself. At the very least, I would have treated her to an image rehab.

I contemplated other lost souls I'd helped. There was Olivia, castaway daughter of Daddy's hotshot client. I helped her see that tattoos, body piercing, and inappropriate boyfriends were not the constructive answer to family strife.

And then there was Tai, who needed the gift of a makeover. And my French cousin Dani, who couldn't see that true love, Jean-Michel, was right in front of her. And our childhood friend, Emily, who needed help communicating with her father. I was such the enabler in all those situations.

What was it about Tara that overrode my helping gene?

I squashed the voice in my head—because it was Amber's. "You don't want to help her. You're threatened by her. She's taking Daddy away. And your room. She's the sister you never wanted."

By dinnertime, I was on ponder overload. I needed to switch gears. To do something proactive, productive. I glanced around my room, and my eye fell on the Rancho Hot Springs brochure. Hello! The weekend was coming up, and I hadn't even made a dent in my to-do list.

I'd just gotten started when Daddy knocked at my door. I looked up and smiled, picturing a bonding moment. Could Daddy not be carrying a tray with my dinner, smiling benevolently? Would we not fully stumble all over each other, me apologizing, him forgiving?

It was the mother of all not evens.

Daddy was furiously tray- *and* forgiveness-challenged. He didn't take even one baby step into my room but hovered in the doorway. "I see you have the Rancho Hot Springs brochure out. Good. I stopped in to tell you I've made a decision about it."

Unwelcome news alert. Daddy informed me of a heinous change in the agenda. He and I were no longer going alone to Rancho Hot Springs, as planned. It would now be a "family" thing. Him, Melissa, me, and Tara.

I was stunned. I stammered, "Even after what just happened? In spite of the fact that forcing Tara on me clearly is not a good plan? I mean, Daddy, you didn't even give me a chance to explain about Saturday night."

Daddy veered into the parent-hood. "I don't want to hear it. Melissa and I have made our decision. We need to spend some time together, all four of us. As the family we're going to be."

Full gloom descended. Black, the way my room would be if Tara got it. Daddy continued. "I've already changed our reservation. We leave Friday after school. This is nonnegotiable, Cher, so don't bother trying."

Before turning away, Daddy added, "Your dinner's on the table. I suggest you eat it before it gets cold."

As if I could even be hungry.

Instead, another feeling came over me. Totally out of nowhere, I was suddenly seized with a raging need to unearth my archival kindergarten drawings. The ones De had taunted me about in the halcyon days BT: before Tara. The ones I'd started to look for when I got side-barred about how overstuffed and undercatalogued my closet was.

I dragged the step stool over to reach the higher elevations of my closet shelves. And that's where I found them, hidden deep inside a pink Barbie suitcase. Okay, so in retro? I was such not the art prodigy. The Crayola colors were best described as primitive. And the outfits? Lame Barbie copies.

But my perceptive t.b. De *had* nailed the subtext. Maybe those drawings weren't about fashion after all. Maybe they did express my yearning for a big family. Copying the classic *Brady Bunch* sibling staircase pose, I'd captioned each portrait, "Cher's sisters. This is Courtney, the oldest. Elizabeth comes next. I'm the middle sister." Then I mixed my sitcom metaphors as the *Full House* influence reared its redundant head: "And these are the twins, Ashley and Mary-Kate."

Poring over the drawings connected me with my inner only child. The one who, I guess, once wished for siblings. Interpretation? I should be welcoming Tara. The concept of her anyway.

So why wasn't I? I mean, so okay, she's totally not the sister I dreamed of having. But like that famous poem, "If you can't be with the one you drew, accept the one you're stuck with."

And that's when it sank in. With a thud. As De said, "Accept it. And move on."

I relocked the pictures in the Barbie suitcase and shoved them back on the shelf. Then, I made a mental note of the exact time and day. This is the moment I'm going to accept Tara. I'm going to move on and take her with me. I am going to make this work. For Daddy. For Melissa. For all of us. She's going to be my . . . stepsister. I'm going to win her over. It's what I do. It's me.

Then I looked around. She's never getting my room.

Just then, my phone rang. De fully commiserated with my incarceration. "First, your dress gets trashed. Then your Manolos get stomped. Now you're grounded? All because of Tara. I'm offended for you."

Calmly, I countered, "No, De, it's okay. I mean, it *is* her fault, but I've done some serious mulling. And revelation? You were right. Nothing lasts forever. I've got to accept her. I've got to win her over."

De was beyond impressed. "I so bow to the altar of your generous nature. To rise above your own feelings of ambiguity? To pledge allegiance to the snarky stepsib to be? You are the best. I'm going to miss my virtual sister."

My jaw dropped. "Hello! You're *not* losing a virtual sister. You're gaining . . . well, okay, I'm not sure what yet. But nothing will ever change our relationship, Dionne Davenport. You were there before Tara."

De sighed deeply. I knew what she was thinking. "Before Tara. Before Richard. That was then . . ."

I refused to let her slide into Pity City. Adamantly, I announced, "And this is now. And now we have a mission, girlfriend. It's all Project: Getting Murray Back. Let's discuss amongst ourselves."

De paused. "Unexplored terrain, Cher. I've never had to *work* to get him back."

"New experience, De. Challenge accepted. Together we can accomplish anything. I propose we start tomorrow. In homeroom, have a FedEx delivered from FAO Schwarz with a huge, huggably expensive teddy bear. When you open it, I'll ask—loudly—who it's from. You'll blush and go, 'Philippe.' The next day, in English, we'll do faux flowers from that shopping bag model. The next—"

De interrupted my how-to-make-Murray-jealous vision. "Wake up and smell the latte, Cher. It won't work. I made sure he found out about my dating Jed, Philippe, and Diego. He doesn't care. In case you haven't noticed, he and Sean are muy occupado trolling for twinkies."

Just then the call waiting beeped. My hopes soared. Because I knew it was Murray. Hello, after the way he looked at De today? The patch-up is in the bag.

But when I clicked on, the voice at the other end

was female. As in, Tara. "I figured I wasn't the only one Shawshanked," she explained, "so I might as well call you. Besides, I have news you could use."

Disappointed that it wasn't Murray, I sighed. But in the spirit of my new must-win-her-over decision, I went, "Hang on, Tara. I'm on with De, I'll put us on three-way."

Tara's news-flash *was* "We interrupt this program." Amber had actually honored De's dare. Before grudgingly returning home on Sunday, she'd given Tara the bogus milk carton she'd been sequestering. Early this morning she'd called and hired Melissa to track down the truth.

I was relieved. Correction: amazed. By getting Amber to come to her senses, Tara had accomplished the highly improbable. Yet I couldn't bring myself to give her snaps.

De could, adding, "Since you're on a roll, maybe you can help me figure out this one. I've decided to do something I've never done."

Tara guessed, "Go a day without makeup?"

De let the quasi quip slide. "I'm on a mission to get my boyfriend back. Cher thinks I should make him jealous by sending myself stuff and pretending it's from faux admirers, but—"

Tara snorted. "It hasn't worked, right? What a surprise."

Miffed, I interjected, "And I assume you have a more workable idea?"

Tara sniffed. "Send herself stuff? You think money solves everything, don't you, Cher?"

"Been there, dissed that. If you have a plan, Tara,

just share." Inwardly, I shuddered at what *she* considered boy bait. Hello, this was a girl with a belly ring and shaved head whose idea of kicks was blowing smoke at unsuspecting innocents.

De coaxed, "I'm all ears, Tara."

Tara was all ideas: "Okay, here's what you do. First, the visuals. Is there some outfit you know he loves you in?"

De guffawed. "Yeah, but it's from the Frederick's of Hollywood boutique."

"And what's wrong with that?"

Tara was serious! I couldn't believe it. As she rambled on, she got more obtuse. I mean, her sure-fire advice? It was all that archaic song, "Dress for him. Wear your hair for him." Instead of being over-the-edge, Tara's advice was rampantly reactionary.

De reacted predictably. "I refuse to stoop to that level! That is so anti-girl. Reality check: He's the one who should be stooping."

Tara rejoined, "But he isn't, is he?"

"Look, Tara," I said, "we've come far, far from the days of pretending to be who we're not—wearing our hair a certain way, dressing a certain way—just to get a boy to like us. Have all the articles in *Ms.* magazine been in vain?"

Tara chided, "And *your* plan—covert manipulation—is better?"

In tandem, De and I noted, "It has proved reliable before."

"Whatever," Tara said. "Do it your way. When it still doesn't work, then come back to me. Besides, I really called to facilitate a breakup, not a makeup."

I was perplexed. "Decode, Tara."

When she did, I was sorry I'd asked. "This whole thing between your father and my mother has gone far enough. Whether you choose to admit it or not, I *know* you don't want them to get married, either."

"That's where you're off the hook, Tara." I said it less than convincingly.

And Tara knew it. "I have a proposal: we team up to break them up."

"As if!" I huffed. "How could you even think that?"

"Pul-eeze, Cher. You're thinking it, too. I'm just saying it out loud."

"No, Tara. Even if I do . . . that is, did . . . have doubts about the upcoming nuptials, I would never do anything that deliberately hurtful."

Just before clicking off, Tara tossed in the kicker: "Have it your way, little miss TGIF. I'll have to do it by myself. See you at Rancho Hot Springs!"

Chapter 11

School was called on Friday due to high smog alert. Which led to the kind of trading-'tudes switch that's funny on TV but not in real life: *I* was bummed and *Daddy* was pumped. He jocularly declared, "Now we can get an early start to the weekend!"

Amendment: jump-start to my new reality. Because all four of us would be driving up together, Daddy reminded me I had less trunk room than originally planned. Ergo, fewer Horowitz suitcases would fit. It took me hours to revisit. In the end, I valiantly sacrificed, making do without several cute little poolside outfits and their attending accessories. That's how determined I was to make the family thing work.

Hello, it was more than you could say for Tara. When we drove to the Valley to pick them up—massively out of our way—was she even ready? As if. Daddy had to stand at the door and cool his heels as Tara got a jump on making good on her threat.

Her how-to-break-them-up plan? Totally transparent: She was fully invested in making her mom—and by extension, us—miserable. First, she'd flat-out refused to go. Then, when she lost that battle, she mulishly wouldn't pack. When Melissa threatened to do it for her, she fully dragged her feet getting out of bed and getting ready. It had been temper tantrum city at their house all morning. Hello, how second grade could you get?

By the time they approached our car, mother and daughter were such the case study in conflict. Melissa, who'd aimed for cruisewear casual chic, instead looked like mom overboard: fully frazzled. Tara, who'd chosen environmentally inappropriate hip-hop attire for her debut at the luxurious resort— oversize hooded sweatshirt over biker pants with a stripe down the side—was scowling. At least her brimmed FUBU cap obscured her baldie.

Daddy hauled their suitcases into the trunk. Then he did something woefully out of character. He tapped on my window, motioned with his thumb, and commanded, "Cher, get in the back with Tara." Not "Would you mind?" Or "Sorry, sweetie, do me a favor." Just "Get in the back."

Excuse me? The backseat? Where trendy shopping bags go? And take-out food? I always sit up front. Now I get relegated to kiddie status, while Melissa takes my place? What's that about?

Okay, so I could get pretty second grade, too.

Self-realization is a beautiful thing. I stopped mid-fume and gamely complied. Whatever. Maybe after we'd driven for a while, Tara would defrost.

Maybe she did. I wouldn't know. In one efficient motion, the teen ogre slammed the door and clamped CD headphones on. She turned the volume up so high that I couldn't avoid hearing her musical choice: sledgehammer rock.

I tried to tune her out, but focusing instead on the fraught-with-drama front seat interface was not a positive alternative. Whatever my consoling daddy had to say to sad-eyed Melissa would be total information overload. Sighing, I slipped my own headphones on, searching for an emotionally comfortable zone. But somehow Deepak Chopra's *Quantum Healing* couldn't drown out Sonic Youth. Or Primal Scream.

The freak convergence of backseat accommodations, the visual attack of Tara's ensemble, and the aural assault of her heinous musical choices combined for a deeply distasteful ride. The urge to whip out my cellular and call De—or even Amber—was overwhelming. But my t.b.'s took bonus school holidays as sleep-in excuses. The emptiness of voice mail was all that awaited.

Thankfully, the comfort level changed dramatically as, hours later, we arrived at our destination. The huge sign, Rancho Hot Springs: Because You Deserve It, was profoundly welcoming.

I drank in the surroundings as we drove up the elegant winding entryway. Bordered by an awesome arboretum of pink-blush dogwood trees, jacarandas, and leafy palms, the Rancho was fully ablaze with tulips, daffodils, and hyacinths. Trickling streams ribboned the drive up to the main building. Gleaming sculptures and gurgling fountains added visual oomph. The total picture offered a promise of tranquillity: instant mood elevation.

Okay, so that was short-lived. New reality jolt: Daddy and Melissa took the two rooms that had been originally designated as Horowitz-only. His efforts to reserve two more rooms at such the late date had been brutally rebuffed.

Translation: Tara and I would share. An unexpectedly heinous plot twist.

On the upside, our accommodations were seriously stellar. Our huge room was decorated in state-of-the-art everything: TV, VCR, lushly quilted, pillow-obsessed double beds, marble bath with a glass shower and separate soaking tub. French doors opened onto a tiled lanai, accessorized with svelte teak furniture. Everything was bathed in comfort colors of the Southwest—peach, gauze, and powder blue.

While I admired the landscape, Tara staked out her turf. She claimed the bed closest to the door—planning her escape, no doubt. When she wasn't looking, I put the This Is a Non-Smoking Room sign on her night table.

Tara snagged the top drawer of the dresser and quickly unpacked. She'd gone furiously minimalist, hardly bringing anything. Nobly, I offered, "You can borrow any of my ensembles. I think we're about the same size."

She rebuffed my generosity. "But we hardly have the same taste."

If De were here, she'd note, "That's because you don't have any taste," but I just shrugged. "Whatever. If you change your mind, the offer holds."

Tara eyed me hopefully, "Speaking of offers that hold—jump in anytime to help me break up the over-the-hill love couple."

I was about to adamantly restate my position, but I suddenly thought better of it. Maybe if I knew her plan, more efficient thwarting could ensue. "Just how do you plan to do that, Tara? So far, all I can see is you being defiant, rude, and noncompliant, making your mother miserable. And the shaved head tactic."

Tara grinned with delight, took off her cap, and ran her palm over her now peach-fuzzed pate. "Mom went postal over that one."

I folded my arms. "Debrief, Tara. How exactly is your mother supposed to guess that all this overtly bad behavior is to prevent her from marrying Daddy?"

Tara sneered at me. "I don't play guessing games, Cher. I came right out and told her not to marry him. She's being selfish, because I don't want to be related to him. I hate him. He's a puffed-up, self-important, pretentious overblown bag of wind."

My mouth flew open. I sputtered, "That's way spurious! How could you say that about Daddy? He's totally—"

Just then I heard his voice, accompanied by a rap on the door. "Cher? Tara? You girls done unpacking? May we come in?"

I shot Tara an icy look and marched over to the door.

Daddy and Melissa had already settled in and changed into bathing suits and cover-ups. Still reeling from Tara's explosive Daddy diss, I barely managed to give Melissa props for her choice: a stunning sunning ensemble that whispered low-key luxe.

Daddy, in his navy Polo Sport ensemble, was grinning, "Isn't this amazing? Just a few hours out of LA and no smog at all. The sun is shining, and we've got time for an afternoon dip before dinner. Come join us."

Picturing a natural tanning op calmed me. "Righteous idea, Daddy." Then I spied a familiar large, flat box tucked under his arm. My eyebrows shot up. "You and Melissa are going to play Scrabble?"

Daddy aimed his response at Tara, "Your mom tells me . . . what's that expression? You *rule* at Scrabble. I thought we'd all play together."

I turned away quickly so Daddy wouldn't catch *my* expression—a blend of bewilderment and nausea. We're going to sit by the pool and play a game? Hello, being together is bad enough. Doesn't he know that forcing us to do stuff together is viciously counterproductive?

The pool at Rancho Hot Springs turned out to be a kickin' full-service water salon. It featured an underwater elevator, lounging walls of water, circular conversation pits, and sculpted projectiles frothing and spitting water. Cutting-edge sun-blocking cabanas riddled the area. We were all appropriately awed.

There Tara and I actually stumbled on common ground: pool boy appreciation. It was Speedo city as a flotilla of totally tan, bred-to-be bathing-trunk Baldwins swarmed the pool terrain. The scene inspired a spontaneous gawk-fest.

Unsurprisingly, our flirting styles clashed. While I did the three Cs—coy, casual, controlled—Tara opted for the three Ds: daring, defiant, direct. She practically stuffed our room number into the trunks of one of the towel-bearing hotties.

Daddy and Melissa observed us, amused. They were making themselves comfortable inside a family-size, four-chaise cabana when a contingent of uniformed wait-staff materialized.

"Mr. Horowitz, I assume?" the wiry lead one asked. "Welcome to Rancho Hot Springs. I'm Bruce, I'll be your personal concierge for the duration of your stay. If there's anything I can do to make your visit more pleasant, please don't hesitate to let me know. I see you've already selected a cabana. Can I bring you and your lovely family some refreshments?"

Bad phrasing alert.

Tragically, there was no button I could hit to obliterate Tara's rude response.

She sneered, "We're *not* his lovely family. I'm not related to him. Nor is she." Tara pointed to Melissa, who threw her a sharp silencing stare. Tara, victorious in creating an intensely awkward moment, found a way to make it worse. Maliciously, she

126

added, "You *can* bring me something, though. I'm in the mood to smash something—how 'bout a Sledgehammer?"

Serendipitously, Daddy wasn't eating, because it would have been a Heimlich 911—he would have choked. As it was, he turned purple. Melissa's hand flew to her throat: she gasped.

Instantly, I spin-controlled, loudly announcing, "Tscha! That's the name of a cool, refreshing, trendy drink—I'd like one, too. And by the way"—I eyeballed the concierge—"we're both seventeen. Appropriate ingredients apply."

Bruce grinned. "Two virgin Sledgehammers. Coming up."

I turned to Tara. Two could play this game.

Daddy and Melissa, still shaken, needed a moment. They got up to stroll the grounds—hand in hand, I noted with satisfaction. I settled myself on a lounge chair and slathered sunscreen on my legs. Tara snagged the chaise next to me. "Nice save, Cher—this time. But you're out of your league, Little Miss Rated-G."

I squinted into the sun. "You're right, Tara. Normally, I don't play in this league. But you've left me no choice. So, whatever, Little Miss Rated-R, challenge accepted."

I paused, regarding her. "By the way, I suggest you borrow the sunscreen. A burned scalp is a majorly uncomfortable way to spend the weekend."

In response, Tara grabbed her cap from her beach duffel, pulled it over her eyes, and grumbled, "One question, Cher. Is your perkiness congenital? 'Cause

I'd rather dive headfirst into a vat of my own vomit than catch it."

Only because I was hyper-vigilant about my vow to make this work did I not one-up her. Not because I couldn't.

When Daddy and Melissa returned, they busied themselves setting up the Scrabble game. My body language screamed, *"Bad plan, Daddy!"* Tragically, he didn't interpret but remained steadfast in his scheme to engender togetherness. Before I could object, we were all picking letters.

Melissa had been right. Tara did rule Scrabble— she was such the word wizard! Segue: all the words she formed were furiously negative. To my three-letter *INK*—hello, I got the *K* on triple letter—she skillfully added an *ST* to make *STINK*. To Melissa's *ATE*, she flashed venom at Daddy before prefixing an *H*. Her own words included *TOXIN, EVIL,* and *NASTY*. The once innocent *ITCH* became *WITCH*.

I bowed to her powers of obsession. Like that famous poem, she left no moment unturned to let us know how she felt.

To divert attention from Tara's poison wordplay, I focused on Melissa, mentioning, "I heard you've taken on the case of our least favorite not-missing person."

Daddy's eyebrows shot up. "What case is that?"

Since Daddy was out of the Ambu-loop, Melissa filled him in. "Cher's friend Amber believes she was stolen as an infant. She's hired me."

Daddy laughed, something he hadn't done in

days. "You're kidding, right? I've known the Marins family for years, and there's no way—"

Melissa interrupted him. "But you didn't know them when she was born, did you?"

I saluted Melissa's power of attorney, and so did Daddy, who had to admit that he met the family when both Amber and I were toddlers.

"So you're taking this investigation seriously?" I prompted.

Melissa tilted her head. "I take all my cases seriously. Especially when they involve young people." As Melissa expertly used the *V* from Tara's *EVIL* to form the word *LOVE*, she added, "Of course, I've just begun to investigate. I put in a call to the national missing children's database."

Dinner at Rancho Hot Springs surpassed any culinary fest I'd ever attended. The spa-cuisine menu, which included haute soup, steamed veggies, and poached salmon, was furiously healthy and tasteful. Not that Tara could agree. Displaying her trademark testiness, she refused to eat and sulked until her mother ran out of patience and excused her from the table. "Go to your room, Tara," Melissa ordered, "and stay there. No going out."

Watching her retreating form, I felt an unexpected pang of sympathy—and okay, so it also gave me an excuse to flirt with the studmuffin waiter—I asked for a doggy bag to bring back for Tara. Maybe, removed from Daddy and Melissa, she'd find her appetite. And I'd begin the way daunting task of winning her over.

But like that famous poem about good deeds going unpublished, Tara rebuffed my edibles offering. When I got back to the room, I found her sitting cross-legged on the floor, amid a pile of candy and cookie wrappers. She'd devoured the noxious contents of the mini-bar.

I didn't rebuke her infantile behavior. I wasn't the boss of her. Besides, just then my cellular rang. It was De. She was weakening—she felt compelled to call Murray, so she called me instead. I complimented her reserve. "Being obvious is not what becomes a Betty best. We'll think of something more doable as soon as I get back. Hang in there. And call me every time you need to."

Just as I clicked off, Amber called, livid. She accused us of sneaking out of town. "My attorney takes a vacation—while I'm paying her good money! The Supreme Court will hear about this," she threatened.

"It's the weekend, Amber—even Ruth Bader Ginsburg frees her hair from that bun sporadically. And segue, Melissa's on it. She's already started to investigate your . . . case."

All at once, Amber's rambling, Tara's contriteness, and De's angst felt like emotional weights, dragging me down. I felt cluttered, so I filled the marble-tiled soaking tub for a full cleansing. Just in case De called, I took my phone with me.

On a whim, I called Sean. And hello, he confirmed—after a verbal tirade from me demanding the truth—that maybe Murray wasn't so into Tiffany anymore. Or any other random Betty. That maybe trolling for twinkies was unfulfilling. Like empty calories. Or *Melrose Place*.

While Sean refused to admit what I suspected—hello, Murray was suffering dumper's remorse—he tossed out enough hints. Enough for me to call De and begin to plot.

"What's so wrong about just calling him?" De's naive question could only be asked by the never been humiliated.

"Okay, call him if you must—but vital point: hang up before he answers. That way you'll fulfill your need but won't come off needy."

Reluctantly, De agreed.

When I got out of the tub, Tara was gone. She'd fully defied her mother's stay-in-the-room edict. I was conflicted. Should I tell Melissa? But, hello, how would ratting on her enable me to win her over?

Should I go after her? I was swathed in a plush pink terry RHS robe, my freshly washed hair twirled in a towel. It would take at least a half hour to dry. By which time whatever damage Tara was inflicting would be done.

In the end, exhaustion ruled. I fell into deep slumber.

The phone woke me up. "Good morning, Pumpkin!" Daddy's voice was beyond chipper. "It's a beautiful day—I've reserved a tennis court for 10 A.M."

Groggily, I responded, "That's major, Daddy. Have fun—just don't strain your back serving. You know what can happen—"

He interrupted, "Actually, Cher, I was thinking of a doubles game. You and me against Melissa and Tara. From what Melissa tells me, it'd be a pretty good match-up."

Two thoughts pierced my sleep-addled brain. Daddy just will not cease and desist forcing us to do stuff together. Trying to get him to wake up and smell the disaster was a lost cause.

And . . . I peered over at Tara's bed. At least she was in it—barely. I had no clue when she'd gotten in, but she'd never bothered changing out of her clothes. Or even her scuffed-sole Doc Martens. She was on top of the covers, in the fetal position.

Instead of being annoyed, an unexpected wave of tenderness came over me. "Daddy? Could you change the tennis reservation for, uh, later? Tara's still asleep."

When I got back from a bodacious breakfast, Sleeping Baldie was awake. Still in bed, still fully clothed, bleary eyes wide open. I tried not to appear confrontational. "Hot date last night Tara? Which pool boy was it, bachelor number one, two, or . . ."

Tara grunted, flipped over on her stomach, and buried her face in the pillow.

"No worries, Tara. I didn't tell anyone you pulled an all-nighter."

"Too bad" came her muffled reply.

Impulsively, I perched on the corner of her bed. "I don't know what you did last night, but I do know this. Being such the rebel is viciously counterproductive. You end up only hurting yourself."

Slowly, she rolled over to face me. Her makeup

132

was furiously smeared. "What's it to you, Cher? I didn't smoke in the room. Your precious little lungs are safe."

I sighed. A heart-to-heart was premature. At best. "Daddy's reserved tennis courts. Our presence is requested—for a doubles game. Did you bring tennis attire, or do you want to borrow something?"

Tara snorted. "Chill, Cher. I wouldn't think of embarrassing you by wearing anything from my L'il Kim collection—not on the state-of-the-snob Rancho Hot Springs Har-Tru tennis courts. But watch your back, Goody Two-sneakers, I'm a mean player."

"Color me warned," I replied as I got up to change for the game.

Chapter 12

A half hour later Daddy and I stood facing Melissa and Tara across the tennis court. Tara wasn't bluffing. She *was* a mean tennis player. Accent on the mean. Although, segue: she did own proper attire—of sorts. Tara's Everlast tennis togs were borderline brand-name friendly, if down-market. Her racquet, however, was fully righteous, an oversize Prince.

The match-up was severe. It turned out that tennis was a Hellinger family tradition—not unlike the rounds Daddy and I used to play. In simpler times.

The Hellingers won the toss, and it was Tara's serve. Translation: a moment of Tara power. And she was determined to use it—against everyone. She bounced the ball fully endlessly. Finally, Melissa spun around and hissed under her breath, "Serve it, Tara. Now."

She did. Like that *Die Hard* movie, with a vengeance. Tara tossed the ball up in the air and smacked it with such intense force that it flew by me.

Daddy grinned. "Gotta keep on your toes, Cher. That's fifteen-love."

Gotta . . . excuse me? Keep on my toes? What was it about being in Melissa's and Tara's presence that sent Daddy into sitcom-speak? Whatever. He didn't fare too well under Tara attack, either. The score was thirty-love in a nanosecond. But the next time Tara served to me, I sent it flying back. The ensuing rally lasted for minutes. In spite of my reluctance to even be here, I had to give Daddy and Melissa snaps. In the end, the Hellingers emerged from Game One victorious, but it was a good doubles match-up.

When it was my serve, I picked up the ball. I was just about to toss it into the air when I caught Tara's stare. It was fully malevolent. I had to fight the urge to smash it right past her smirk-plagued face. Tell me again what she's doing here, infringing on my life? My friends' lives? My family? My entire existence?

Suddenly, I got in touch with my inner Venus Williams. I slammed the ball so hard that it wiped the sneer off Tara's face as she dove for it. Heinously, she did manage to return it—just barely. But I'd made her sweat.

"Nice one, Cher!" Daddy beamed. "Though, for future reference, killing the ball is not a requirement." He gently lobbed Tara's shot back over the net toward Melissa. It was a total puff-ball, which she backhanded smoothly in my direction.

I glanced at Tara, who had the nerve to be making

another evil face at me! I rushed toward the ball and smashed it back. This time it whizzed right past the bald eagle. The expression on Tara's face morphed from taunting to fuming. I'd rattled her. She furiously fumbled the ball multi-times during that game. Only Melissa's smooth moves kept it from being a Horowitz sweep, but after a way sweaty ten minutes, the game was practically in the bag. When I nailed the post-deuce point, I couldn't help crowing. Loudly.

"Yes!" I jumped up and shouted. "Advantage— Horowitz!" I was fully revved to put her away, until Daddy shot me a gentle but firm reminder: "Relax, Cher. It's only a friendly doubles game."

As if. "Tell it to Tara," I started to say, but her actions spoke for themselves.

My next serve was to the bad seed. I centered myself, determined to rise above her obnoxious level. I bounced it fully fairly in the center of her quadrant. Tara was also determined—to do me bodily harm. Her rage-fueled return ball went straight for my head. Instinctively, I blocked my so-far original nose by shielding it with my racquet. The ball bounced off it, but tragically, stayed on our side. Instead of the win we should have bagged, grievously, we were at deuce again. Or, as Tara snickered, with her hand on her hip, "Oops, dis-advantage Horowitz."

Melissa whirled around, seething. "A moment. We need a moment."

Then she took Tara off court for a mother-daughter huddle. As Daddy strode over to me, I could see Melissa's face turning red—and not from the sun. Or any physical exertion. It was all angst, courtesy of

Tara, who stood arms crossed in that archival defensive position, feigning boredom.

Daddy rubbed the back of his neck. Signal: Tara's wearing him down—which is just what she wants.

"Cher, this is getting out of hand," he said gently. "I know Tara's not making it easy. But you're letting her bait you. C'mon, sweetie, this isn't you."

"I'm trying," I protested. Daddy didn't know the half of it.

"Try harder," he urged. He glanced at the other side of the court. "Come on, they're ready to play again."

As Melissa and her officious offspring took their positions, I gulped several calming breaths. I chanted my mantra. "I will make this work. I can."

I served to Melissa, who hit the ball back to me. My return shot was aimed at Tara. I accessorized it with a friendly, forgiving, bygones smile. Stubbornly chastised-impaired, she responded with a shot, too—a tennis ball going way above the speed limit, right into my stomach. I doubled over. Daddy rushed toward me. "Are you okay, Cher?"

It was more about being caught off guard than being in actual pain. But Tara had knocked the wind out of me, so it took a minute to regain composure. Eventually, I waved Daddy away, assuring him that I was unharmed. Just startled.

Tara crowed victoriously, *"That's* advantage Hellinger!"

Melissa scowled. "No, that's a do-over, because of your unsportsmanlike behavior." She turned to me. "Cher, please serve it again."

Valiantly, I resisted the urge to go quid pro quo. Instead, I focused. I concentrated on doing the perfect, Martina Hingis–like serve, forceful but fair. Melissa went for it and sent it back at Daddy. A full rally ensued, and eventually Daddy and I won the game. We were even: two games apiece.

As we started game three, I almost relaxed: the worst had to be over.

But not even. The détente didn't last long. It was Melissa's serve, and we were even at thirty-thirty when she hit it to Daddy. He gracefully sent it back— and that's when Tara the terrible struck again. As the ball flew over the net, she rushed up and smashed it back. It was headed toward me, so I backed up to make the shot. Because it was higher than I guessed, I had to dash all the way to the outer limits of the court to return it. Summoning Xena strength, I whirled it back.

Tara was ready. She was at the net, waiting. She never let the ball bounce on their side. She merely held her raquet up, right in the path of the oncoming ball—and tipped it lightly over the net. Daddy never had a chance at it. Nor did I. It dropped like a dead weight an inch over the net, on our side.

"Forty-thirty," Tara crowed. "Ready for us to put you away?"

"As if," I snarled, taking my place on the court. Melissa served to me, and I handled it easily, sending the ball back to her. But Tara, eyeing Daddy malevolently, suddenly bolted in front of her mother. Profound premonition alert! She was going to hurt Daddy! Just as she sent the ball hurtling toward him,

I rushed in front of him and smacked it back at her. Correction: smacked it right past her.

With furiously faux admiration, Tara drawled, "Oooh, stealth poaching. Any other hidden talents we should know about, Cher?"

I huffed, "Excuse me, what's good for the goose is good for the duck pâté. You did it first before, when you raced in front of your mother to purposely inflict grievous injury on us. Which you were about to do to—"

Daddy was steaming. He'd had it. "Okay. That's it!" he thundered. "You two want to act like children, that's how you'll be treated. You both need a time-out! Go to your room and stay there until you've worked out your issues. All of them. I don't want to see you, or hear from you, until you can at least be civil to each other. And to us. Got it?"

Excuse me? *I* was being incarcerated—with Tara? Merely for standing up for myself? For protecting pater? I turned an unflattering shade of scarlet as I whined, "But, Daddy, that's not fair. I have been trying. It's her, not me. This is beyond human."

Melissa interjected, "Tara, you heard Mel. This is getting ridiculous. To your room *now*, young lady. Do not come out until you've apologized to Cher and worked this out."

Hel*lo*! At least Melissa knew I was such the offended party.

Tara flung her pricey tennis racquet to the ground and stormed away.

Daddy turned on his heel. "Go, Cher. I mean it. This has gone far enough."

I was steaming. Fully aboil!

I dragged my Nike heels on the way back to our room. I tried to go Zen, to becalm myself. I stopped to smell the flowers. I took refuge on a bench. Until Daddy spied me, and ordered me to stop dawdling.

I half-expected Tara to be AWOL when I got to the room. But grievously, she'd acquiesced to her mother's orders. She was kneeling by the mini-bar, extracting a bottle of a not immediately identifiable liquid.

Noting the horrified look on my face, she smirked. "Relax, Cher. It's iced tea."

"Excellent," I rejoined, flopping on my bed. "Maybe it'll help you chill out."

"Me? What about you? Looks like Totally Tennis Barbie came a little undone out there."

I was sweating. Tara's cold drink looked inviting. I hopped off the bed and crouched over her shoulder to check out the selection. I snagged a bottled water and pressed it against my forehead. Such the simple pleasure in life. Then I guzzled it thirstily.

Tara was staring at me. She backed up onto her bed.

I took a deep breath and tried—again—for rapport. "Tara, we have to deal with this. We are going to have to coexist under the same roof. We are, I guess, going to be stepsisters, and—"

"Not if I can help it," she snarled.

"That's just it, Tara," I said as gently as I could. "You can't help it. So you might as well accept it. Including me. I sort of come with the package."

Tara flushed with anger—and then delivered a

way harsh blow. "Accept you? Why? So I can live the nightmare of having the ultimate Marcia Brady as a stepsister? It isn't going to happen, Cher. Let me spell this out for you. I don't even want to know you, let alone be quasi-related to you. I don't want to go to your school, be with your friends, sleep in your room. I never even wanted to meet you! I don't want you, your money, or any of your stupid clothes! We were doing fine without you!"

Tara's emerald eyes flashed venom.

But I saw the hurt.

Just then my cellular rang. It was De, mid-Murray crisis. Her voice quavered, but she was determined—to do the wrong thing. "I'm going to his house. I'm going to confront him, Cher, tell him I miss him. I'm just going to swallow my pride and do it. And nothing you can say can stop me."

Keeping my eyes on Tara, I exhaled and said calmly, "Bad plan, De. You should never swallow your pride. Don't go to his house."

Surprisingly, Tara leaped off the bed and motioned to me to give her the phone. "Dionne? This is Tara. Look, here's the plan. Snag two tickets for the Lakers—they're playing the Knicks tonight. I know it's last minute, but money will buy anything. Then go to his house, tickets in hand. He won't be able to resist."

I pulled the phone away from Tara and scolded, "De is not a sports fan. Why should she subject herself to unwelcoming benches, loud buzzers, and the proximity of sweaty athletes? And, segue: Murray will be so into the game, he won't even know she's there. The whole thing will be an exercise in point-lessness."

To De, I advised, "Nix on the Knicks tix. Drive by his house with the top down on your car, chin up, with your hair streaming in the wind . . ."

Tara rolled her eyes and turned away. I clicked off with De.

"You don't know anything," she said quietly.

Suddenly, I was moved to ask her, "Do you have a boyfriend, Tara?"

Without answering, she strode over to the French doors and stepped out onto the patio. I followed and repeated the question.

Sinking into one of the teak lounge chairs, she responded, "Not right now."

"But you did," I coaxed. "Someone special?"

She shrugged. "What's special? Nothing lasts for-ever."

I countered, "That's way cynical, Tara. What about Arnold and Maria? Oprah and Stedman? Dennis Rodman and himself?"

Tara took a long sip of her drink. "Don't change the subject. Like I was saying, my mother and I were doing fine, before you and your fatuous father came along."

I dropped into the chair next to her and pulled over a hassock. We both put our feet up. Carefully, I said, "I'm sure that's true, Tara. Maybe you were doing fine—Club Metro encounters aside—but whatever. What about Melissa? How was she doing?"

"My mother—not that it's any of your business—

was fine. She didn't need Mel Horrorface on his white horse to come rescue her."

The vision of Daddy on a horse gave me pause. A white Mercedes maybe. I considered. "It's not that Daddy was wilting away without her, either. But you'd have to be fully sight-challenged not to see how blissful they are together. Daddy goes around the house whistling! And he's not as obsessed with work. The relationship is doing wonders for his immune system. What about your mother?"

Tara flung her arm over her face and admitted, "She whistles that sappy 'The Way We Were' all the time. I can't stand it."

I bit my lip. "That's why I think maybe they're right, they do belong together. They're following their bliss."

Tara eyed me suspiciously and spat, "Spare me the martyr speech. Like you don't mind that suddenly you'll have a mother running the show. Telling you what to do. Taking away your father. A mother you barely know."

The vision of me in the backseat of Daddy's car came to me. A vision of new decor at Casa Horowitz. Resolutely, I clicked it off.

Reasonably, I countered, "Okay, I know. It'll be adjustment city. But if I had to choose a stepmom? Could I do better than Melissa? Not even."

Tara wasn't buying it. "Truth or dare, Cher. You feel the same exact way I do. You were perfectly content with the way things were. You got everything you wanted out of your father. A situation that's bound to change with Mom in charge. You don't want them to get married any more than I do."

Okay, so like my mouth opened. A million protests came out—silently.

The silence was broken by the phone. De again. She'd called Telecharge and snagged the Laker tickets. And was about to race over to Murray's house.

I had to stop her. I barked, "Give the tickets to your brothers. And . . . and . . ." I had to think fast. "Have flowers addressed to you, but delivered to his house by faux mistake." Okay, I knew that was lame, but I was on trauma-overload with Tara right now and it was the best I could think of.

Rudely, Tara snagged the phone away from me. "De? It's me, Tara. Okay, so after you invite him to the basketball game—tell him about the Jim Carrey marathon in Westwood. Uh-huh—of course you go with him. That's the point."

My eyes flashed angrily. Hello, she's not De's main, *and* she's leading her furiously off course. I wrested the phone from her. Forcefully, I went, "Not even, Dionne. Write yourself an adoring E-mail. Sign it 'Philippe.' Then accidentally forward it to Murray." I clicked End before Tara could intrude again.

She was staring at me. Expecting an answer to her Truth or Dare question.

Finally, I managed to stammer. "I—I—I guess I might feel the same way. Sort of. Deep down. But sometimes we have to do what's best for others. Especially when the others are—"

Tara didn't let me finish. Jarringly, she vaulted off the chair and flew back into the room. She just missed smashing me in the slammed door. Her aim was true, however, with her words: "What's best for others? I'll tell you what's best for my mom. What's best for my mom is to get back with my dad!" Tara screamed and balled her fist. She hadn't touched me, but I fell back on the bed with as much force as if she had.

I was fully shaken. I hadn't taken that into account. That—mother of all duhs—she doesn't even have anything personal against me or Daddy. She just sees us as getting in the way of her goal: bringing her parents back together.

"Is that even within the realm of possibility, Tara?" I inquired softly.

"It was—before you and your stupid father arrived on the scene."

I let the Daddy diss slip. "Do you really think your mother would fall for my father if she was considering a marital rematch with your dad? Haven't they been divorced for a year? Isn't it over?"

Tara fought hard, but finally she caved. She couldn't stop the river of tears from flowing. Soon earthquake-force sobs wracked her body.

Again, that wave of tenderness enveloped me. Especially when she wailed, "I want them back. I want my family back. I want my life back. It isn't fair!"

I squashed the voice in my head that said, "Hello, ditto."

The phone rang again. This time Tara dove for it. But instead of barking at De, Tara, through her sniffles, offered, "I thought of something else. When

145

this, uh, friend of mine was trying to get this boy, she wrote him a letter. It was easier to put her feelings down on paper than to just, you know, blurt them out. So she wrote him this note. It was simple, to the point, honest. Then she sealed it and delivered it—in a tin of homemade brownies."

After listening to De's response, Tara sniffled, "Do you want the recipe?"

Tara paused. Then she said, "Yes, I'm sure your housekeeper can do it. Uh-huh. Okay, write this down."

Instinctively, I knew Tara was talking about herself—not some friend. I thought of that archival but effective Betty Cooker poem: the way to a hottie's heart is through his tummy. I had to give Tara kudos.

Post script: I had to rethink her. Looks and attitude can deceive. Potentially, she's not just a teen ogre who mowed her hair into oblivion, flaunts a belly ring, and blows smoke in innocent people's eyes in grungy rest rooms. Beneath the surface, she could be such the hurt little lamb. She misses her dad. She misses her old life. No wonder she's massively invested in preventing a Daddy-Melissa alliance.

When Tara had given De the last getting-Murray-back ingredient, I gently took the phone from her. "You know what, De? That, uh, sounds like an endorseable plan. Go for it, girlfriend."

I clicked off and sat on the corner of the bed next to Tara. "What you just told De . . . about snagging this boy. It was you, right?"

Tara nodded and sighed.

"So did it work? Did you get the boy?"

Tara's eyes were still moist. "No, but not because my tactics were wrong. It didn't work out because . . ."

"He wasn't the one?"

Tara stared up into space and heaved a major sigh. "I wasn't the one, Cher. See, it's not about finding the right person. It's about *being* the right person. And at that time . . . it was just after my dad moved out. I wasn't myself."

Profound perception alert! Only it didn't sound like something Tara had figured out on her own. As if she could read my mind, she added, "A very smart person taught me that—my mother."

"Look, Tara, I don't pretend to know what happened between your parents. But I would hazard a guess they tried to make it work. I mean, hello, your mom is totally a special person."

Tara folded her arms defensively across her chest. "That's why she should go back with my dad."

"That's why," I countered, "she deserves to follow her bliss. And whether or not either of us wants to accept it, her relationship with Daddy has sent her into the joy zone."

Tara croaked, "Her happiness? What about mine? Don't I count? How could she do this to me?"

"Sometimes"—I bit my lip—"I guess we have to realize that it's not about us."

Like, epiphany.

Thoughtfully, I added, "If you give it a chance, you'll see that just because Daddy and I have a lot of stuff doesn't mean we're bad people. Just like . . .

just because you, uh, smoke, and do all that shock-value stuff doesn't make you a bad person."

Through her veil of tears, Tara sniffled. "I don't even like to smoke. It makes my breath reek."

"Not to mention it's got that carcinogenic thing going," I noted.

Tara shrugged. "I know. I just do it . . . I don't know, for an image thing."

"I think your image should reflect who you are, Tara. The person you really are. It's like that famous poem, 'Advice-giver, heal thyself.' I mean, *being* the right person—isn't that what you just said?"

Revelation: Daddy was brilliant. His decree that Tara and I share a cell worked. Somewhere, in the course of our Shawshank, we inexplicably bonded. We shared, and in that sharing, we cleansed. For Tara, it was like this weight came sliding off her shoulders. It freed her to at least consider the possibility that maybe it would be okay for all of us to be a family.

And like, ditto. Confessing all my confused emotions to the only person who could understand—Tara!—was cleansing. Like a mud wrap.

We spent the whole night in. The resort's Spectra Vision had righteous movies. We watched, we snacked, we continued to share. Tara admitted that her night "out"? She had started to hang with the Speedo-studmuffin towel boys, but they turned out to be brain dead. She got bored and spent the night by the pool, under a lighted cabana, reading a book.

So much for being a wild child.

By the time Daddy and Melissa poked their heads in to check on us, we'd ordered a room service tub of popcorn and were camped out on the floor, in our pj's, watching movies. They were speechless, fully flummoxed.

The next day Tara spent the morning alone with Melissa. Educated guess? They both had a lot to say.

Daddy and I did our version of quality time. We played a stellar game of singles tennis and then lunched at Rancho's poolside café. Daddy gave me deserved snaps. "I don't know what you did, Cher, but it seems to have worked. You won Tara over. Melissa and I . . . well, honey, we couldn't be more thrilled. You're amazing."

I beamed. "I inherited the amazing gene from you, Daddy."

He gazed at me gently. "And from your mother."

That's when I knew that Daddy's marrying Melissa wouldn't change anything important. He would always love her and me. And now Melissa— and Tara—too.

Later Tara and I hit the spa. As advertised, it was profound pampering, with healthful, New Age bene- fits. We got massaged, mud masqued, and detoxified via a thermal seaweed wrap. Tara took to the spa encounter like a natural, sighing, "You know, if this is what life as Cher's stepsister is all about, maybe I can deal. After all."

The weekend had gone from heinous to righteous. As we packed the car to leave, I insisted on sitting in the back with Tara. This time neither of us took out portable CD players. Instead, we played Scrabble.

Tara fully wiped the board with me. But how could I be bugged? Especially after she sacrificed two *S*'s to form *SISTER*.

Just before we hit the L.A. county limits, I turned to her. "We do have one unresolved issue. About my room . . ."

Tara grinned and slipped her headphones on. "Don't want it. Never did."

I slapped her five.

Chapter 13

I hadn't felt this invigorated in weeks. Like my emotional smog had lifted and life was back to bodacious. Thanks mostly to Tara's advice—and her brownies—De and Murray were patched.

"I sat down and keyboarded that letter," De informed me. "I never knew how cathartic that could be."

Totally. For the first time, De was, like, forced to actually *think* about Murray. And like that famous poet, she went all "How do I love thee, let me E-mail the ways." As she typed, it came spilling out of her: a fully heartfelt cyber confession session ensued. De extolled Murray's multi-virtues and let him know how stellar he truly is.

"I hope you told him that he doesn't have to measure up to Richard," I mentioned.

"Tscha! Murray has it all over the cubic zirconium

cousin"—De giggled—"especially when you take Richard's rancid personality into account."

When Murray read De's E-mail, he melted. And when he took his first bite of Tara's brownie recipe, it was all over. He came flying over to De's house, ready to reconcile. They went to the Lakers game. Amazingly, Murray barely watched the on-court action. He was too busy spilling his own true feelings to De. In spite of the eardrum-splitting buzzers and proximity of sweaty athletes, De heard Murray's admission loud and clear. He'd taken Richard's advice because it sounded right—even if it didn't feel right. What he felt, after a slew of random dates, was serious dumper's remorse. But crawling back to De was too pride-piercing to contemplate. "That takes the kind of courage I don't have. But you do, baby. You're the total package: brains, beauty, style, compassion, and courage." Murray had added, "If a babe like you could fall for me? Hey, I must be pretty special."

De had answered, "You are, Murray. I've always known that."

And after the game—instead of hitting the Jim Carrey marathon? The patched pair took in a special midnight showing of *Titanic*. "But we missed the whole sinking part," De added with a wink.

Reuniting with De had a stylistic fringe benefit: Murray remorphed back from khaki to tacky.

So had his best bud. Effervescent Sean, who thought Murray's single-status would be a boon for *his* dating life, came to realize the duh-head error of that illogic. Deep down, Sean knows what I do:

Murray and De totally get each other. They're soul mates.

All was right in our enclave. With the noted exception—doy—of Ambu-lunatic. The drama queen continued to enshroud herself in grievous disguises, still convinced she was being sought by phantom parents. When we returned to school on Monday, Amber was in a short, spiky wig and Hugo Boss suit.

When I passed her in the hallway, I appraised, "Are you getting in touch with your inner Ellen—or did you misinterpret the menswear statement at Milan? It's adapting the *concept* of business suits—not raiding your father's closet."

Amber glanced around furtively and stage-whispered, "What part of *Mulan* didn't you get, Cher? I'm incognito as a boy."

I could not even respond to that. Whatever. As soon as Melissa's investigation was over, Amber would have to find some other delusion to obsess over. I had no doubt that she would.

Tara and I continued to bond cellularly. We talked like three times a day. The more we shared, the more we realized that, despite our wildly divergent styles, tastes in music, and propensity for body piercing, we had so much in common. Starting with: the studmuffin situation. Though both of us had a slew of exes to compare, neither had a special hottie of the moment. And as I sussed the night of the sleep-over, she, too, was Ally McBeal–obsessed. That, Nick at Nite, and the Food Network were her TV choices.

And hello, it turned out that Tara's comfort level at Club Metro had been way exaggerated. "I only went there to freak out my mother," she admitted. "I wanted her to find out."

"Just for the satisfaction of causing her emotional strife?" I asked.

"No," Tara said quietly. "I was hoping she'd be wigged enough to, you know, have to call my father. After all, the one thing they do still have a common interest in is me."

Tara didn't have to verbalize the rest of her thought. I got it. Her fantasy was that in the course of co-parenting, her parental units might coexist again.

"I knew it was a long shot, but when my mom started dating your dad, I got desperate."

"I fully understand, Tara, desperate measurements and all that."

Like that famous platitude, however, today was totally the first day of the rest of a shiny new stellar existence. Tara's current focus was getting up to speed academically for her upcoming enrollment at Bronson Alcott. I pledged to tutor.

I was feeling so majorly psyched during the post-Rancho week, I barely noticed that Daddy's demeanor had shifted ever so slightly. I should have known something was askew when all whistling ceased and desisted.

Yet I took it as a good sign when on Sunday Daddy decreed an instant replay of our backyard barbecue.

"Excellent, pater! This time, I want to extend our

barbecue largesse to all my t.b.'s, Murray, De, Sean, and even Amber."

Another clue missed: Daddy's "Sure, Cher, whatever you want" was recited fully absently.

I plunged forward into setup mode. My freshly minted t.b.-sister-to-be Tara arrived early to help me set up. Okay, so our decorating styles were so not compatible. I went for the visuals of crystal and Chinese lanterns; she insisted on the aural clash of Puff Daddy and goth rock as the musical sound track. Mental note: on a going forward basis, we should just rotate doing stuff like this.

As we worked side by side—me in a sensuous layering of printed chiffon over solid top over capris; Tara in overalls and babydoll T-shirt—I felt a true confession coming on. As those childhood drawings had suggested, I could more than accept having a sister. I could totally get into it. Stepsister, I mean. Especially since she wasn't going to paint my room black. Compromise: she could do whatever she wanted with the west wing.

The barbecue was a raging success. Over turkey burgers, kabobs, and Melissa's killer three-alarm chili, Tara, De, Amber, and I plotted at how to get back at Richard. We decided to print a bumper sticker for his car: "Knows Chelsea. And several other borderline tacky neighborhoods in NYC."

In the middle of our high five, I suddenly blurted to Tara, "You know, with your natural looks, I'd do Meg Ryan over Gwen. Or"—I tilted my head and squinted for better visualization—"you could do a

Dharma with your hair! The whole, tousled, jaunty, I-don't-care hair look. It's not only way classic, it's fully you."

De agreed, but Tara looked doubtful. So I added, "And, uh, in case you missed this month's *Vogue*, news flash: Gwen is over the ragamuffin look. After she met Donatella at a New York fashion show, she admitted, and I quote, 'I think I'm beginning to accept designers.' Deep thoughts, Tara. And happily? The designer-obsessed, valet-parking enhanced Beverly Center is conveniently located within minutes of your new home."

Tara squiggled uncomfortably. "Not so fast, Cher. I'm not going to turn into you, just because we're about to be related. I still need—"

"To be you," I finished, nodding. "I fully agree. Not Gwen. Not Meg. Not even Dharma. You."

Just then Melissa sidled up to us and slipped her arm around Tara's waist. "I just called into my voice mail. There was an interesting message." She focused on Amber. "It settles your case."

Amber, whose barbecue ensemble consisted of a Rampage vintage dress accessorized with a red feather boa, turned white. She gulped. Moment of truth. De and I knew Amber well enough to interpret her body language. Total terror: She looked like Drew Barrymore in the original *Scream*.

So it was major sigh of relief all around when Melissa delivered the bombshell: the milk carton doppelganger was not—like, duh—Amber.

Melissa elaborated. "There's more wonderful news. That girl is no longer missing. Her parents have found her and she's back with them. Isn't that great? As for you, Amber Marabelle Marins . . ."

"Marabelle!" De and I screeched so loud that we drowned out Puff Daddy and his entire extended family. We doubled over with laughter. De was guffawing so hard that her eyes watered, causing massive mascara migration.

Pointing at Amber, I yelped, "Marabelle, we hardly knew ye!"

Amber flushed crimson. It matched her boa. "I changed that heinous middle name legally."

Melissa, bemused, shrugged. "My investigations are pretty thorough, Amber. In fact, I know what you did last summer." She pointed to her nose.

Amber tensed. "That's enough! I've heard enough. Thank you for your time. You'll be well compensated for your efforts."

Melissa strode over and put her arm around Amber's rigid shoulders. "I have a better idea. I don't want your money, Amber, but I do know a worthy organization that could use it."

Amazingly, Melissa convinced Amber to write a check to the Center for Missing and Exploited Children.

Melissa, such the crusader for the rights of the downtrodden, had struck a victory. She'd totally tricked Amber into doing something good.

Engulfed with contentment, I refocused on doing what I do best: planning. And not a moment too soon. Daddy and Melissa hadn't set a date, but, hello, they had no clue how long it takes to produce the perfect Event Wedding.

I lugged my laptop outside, and after dinner, while De and Murray danced, and Sean and Amber consulted a deck of tarot cards, Tara and I worked on the guest list. *And* our daughters of the bride and groom ensembles. We had to decide on color schemes, themes, and gazebo-enhanced locations. For research, I'd snagged the issue of *LA* magazine with the Top 5 Country Clubs.

It was several hours before I realized Daddy and Melissa weren't even here. After dinner, they'd retreated inside. But not, as it turned out, for the lovey-dovey reason anyone would imagine.

It was 10 P.M. when Daddy and Melissa reemerged. I know, because I checked my jaunty barbecue-friendly Swatch timepiece. That's when Daddy signaled for me to shut the music off.

"Melissa and I have an announcement," he said, his arm encircling his intended's waist. They made such the stellar old-people couple.

I fully tingled! They've set the date! Excellent! Now, we can scope those top five country clubs, gather swatches, and interview professional wedding planners. It will be the most righteous nuptials 90210 has seen since Brandon and Kelly. And, brainstorm! We'll hire the L.A. Philharmonic, and they'll play "The Way We Were," the song Daddy and Melissa whistle!

I looked up. The sky was a patchwork of tsuris clouds and those twinkly pink-tingled stars. I glanced at Tara, wanting to share the moment. Her eyes had welled with tears. But, curiously? They weren't the joyous kind. I checked out Murray, De, Amber, and

Sean: they were all staring at me, eyes wide, mouths agape.

What's that about? I emerged from my daydream to focus on Daddy.

". . . so that's why," he was saying, "Melissa and Tara will be leaving for New York next week."

Excuse me? "What . . ." My laptop crashed to the ground as I bolted over to Daddy, stammering, "I think . . . I . . . might've missed something . . . in the translation."

Melissa's eyes filled with tenderness. "What your father just said, Cher, is that I got a job offer in New York, and, well, it's a tremendous opportunity for me to do what I've always wanted, run an organization that represents the underprivileged."

My jaw dropped. "But . . . but . . . I thought . . . what you wanted was . . . us."

Melissa brushed a flyaway strand of hair out of my eyes. "It is. I do. Make no mistake, Cher. I love your father—and you—very much. The timing of this whole thing could not have been worse."

"When did you find out?" I mumbled.

Daddy responded, "She got a call on Monday, when we got back from the resort. We've . . . the two of us, together . . . have spent all week trying to figure out what to do. Believe me, Cher, we've looked at this thing from all angles. This is not something Melissa can pass up. She just can't."

A major icky feeling enveloped me. Especially when I glanced over my shoulder at Tara. She was such the photo of forlorn: her chin cupped in her hands, she was staring, dewy-eyed, into space.

Melissa gave me a gentle peck on the cheek and went over to her.

Dessert was fully bittersweet. Tara's brownies were way excellent, but they got stuck in my teeth. What if I never had them again? I felt like I was losing the only sister I almost had. Moment of honesty: almost didn't want. It was all so bewildering. Like Robert Urich still being on TV.

Then I thought about Daddy. Hello, this wasn't about me.

After everyone left, he and I cleaned up in silence. Finally, I blurted, "I know some excellent elixirs for broken hearts. Deepak Chopra has just come out with a tape . . ."

Daddy tossed me a halfhearted smile. "Cher? Come sit down for a minute. I know this is a bombshell for you, but obviously I've had all week to think about it. And you know, honey, as strange as this might seem? I'm upset, of course, but I'm not—how would you put it—totally bummed?"

I blinked. "You're not? Is it because of that whole 'If you love something, set it free' bumper sticker?"

Daddy sighed. "I'm not sure what you mean. But when Melissa and I sat down and really hashed this out, we needed to be really honest with each other. We had to admit that maybe we rushed into everything a little too soon. Maybe, in our euphoria at finding each other again, after all this time, we just dove in when we should have tested the waters a little longer. Maybe her getting this opportunity is a good thing."

"So, you're not bummed, you're relieved?"

"I wouldn't say relieved, Cher. Melissa and I do have something real together. But if she doesn't try this job, she'd always wonder if she gave it up for me. And I wouldn't want that. Besides, if it's meant to be, she'll be back. In fact, we made a pact. She's going to give it six months. If she's not happy, or if she feels this was a mistake, she'll come back. Hey, we waited thirty years, what's another six months?"

Wisdom and patience: such the grown-up traits. I hugged Daddy.

I couldn't go to bed without calling Tara. She and I had been too stunned to confer about this latest parental shocker.

Predictably, Tara's emotions were massively mixed. Upside: she'd sort of gotten what she'd been wishing for—her father was in New York, and with this relocation, she'd be able to see him every day. Downside: she was as bummed as I was. She'd accepted Daddy as a father figure and me as stepsib. And as she'd realized beneath her mud masque at the spa, she could fully deal with her new life. Now on hold.

"We can still E-mail," I said, trying to be optimistic.

"You better! Cher, I still need your help. I mean, New York—eeeck! Will you help me acclimate and even, you know, shop? I need you."

"We'll go tomorrow," I pledged. "You'll need an entire new wardrobe. I mean, hello, the styles in New York are so totally not like here. I'll make a list.

We will not send you to the Big Apple unprepared. You have my word on that."

There was this long pause. Then, Tara whispered, "Thanks, sis . . . that is, Cher."

"Tscha! You had it right the first time. Maybe we never got to be real sisters, but under the skin, hello, total connection. And that's what counts."

About the Author

Randi Reisfeld is the author of the *Clueless* novels *Dude with a 'Tude, Chronically Crushed, True Blue Hawaii, Too Hottie to Handle, Cher Goes Enviro-Mental, Cher's Furiously Fit Workout,* and *An American Betty in Paris.* She has also authored *Prince William: The Boy Who Will Be King; Who's Your Fave Rave? 40 Years of 16 Magazine* (Berkley, 1997); and *The Kerrigan Courage: Nancy's Story* (Ballantine, 1994), as well as several other works of young adult nonfiction and celebrity biographies. The *Clueless* series, duh, is totally the most chronic!

Ms. Reisfeld lives in the New York area with her family. And, grievously, the family dog.

Sabrina The Teenage Witch™

#1 Sabrina, the Teenage Witch
#2 Showdown at the Mall
#3 Good Switch, Bad Switch
#4 Halloween Havoc
#5 Santa's Little Helper
#6 Ben There, Done That
#7 All You Need is a Love Spell
#8 Salem on Trial
#9 A Dog's Life
#10 Lotsa Luck
#11 Prisoner of Cabin 13
#12 All That Glitters
#13 Go Fetch
#14 Spying Eyes
Sabrina Goes to Rome
#15 Harvest Moon
#16 Now You See Her, Now You Don't
#17 Eight Spells A Week
#18 I'll Zap Manhattan
#19 Shamrock Shenanigans
#20 Age of Aquariums
#21 Prom Time
#22 Witchopoly
#23 Bridal Bedlam
#24 Scarabian Nights

Based on the hit TV series
Look for a new title every other month.

From Archway Paperbacks
Published by Pocket Books

1345-11